A WITCHES OF WYLDEDEN
NOVELLA

A DREAM OF THORNES AND SUNFLOWERS

ALEX CLIFFORD

E-book: ISBN: 978-0-6454799-4-2

Paperback: ISBN: 978-0-6454799-3-5

Alex Clifford

www.alexclifford.com.au

spcafcs@gmail.com

ALSO BY ALEX CLIFFORD

THE WITCHES OF WYLDEDEN CHRONICLES

NOVELLAS

TRYCE POINT BAY

Erve

Diraðale

Rothvale

Phara

Ahrenhale

QIRI

Nir

Yvar

A DREAM OF THORNES AND SUNFLOWERS

A WITCHES OF WYLDEDEN NOVELLA

ALEX CLIFFORD

TW/CW AVAILABLE ON AUTHOR WEBSITE

MIDNIGHT

HAPPINESS WAS NOT A DESTINATION ONE TRAVELED TO, YET, IF it were, Kailevi thought it might be the bedroom he shared with Ellissa Nemuse.

The manor was midnight-quiet, the open window bringing only the sounds of Wyldeden's nighttime fauna feasting on the dandelions everblooming in the field. So many of his sleepless nights had once been spent staring at the stars, memorizing their constellations and praying to the moon, but recent years had given him something much more wondrous to worship.

Sitting in bed, covers twisted around their ankles, Kailevi and Ellissa stared at the weeks-old infant nestled against her chest, suckling lazily. Their daughter had the same sun-kissed coloring as her mother, her big brown eyes light and warm. Amber had always been his favorite gemstone, formed in trees rather than stone. Since his first day at the academies, he'd been drawn to it. Now, every time he met Ellissa's adoring gaze, every time he stared into his daughter's trusting face, he understood why.

"Kai," Ellissa whispered, nodding to the ajar door.

Amber peered through the gap, blinking owlishly.

"Hey, buddy," Kailevi said, swinging his legs out of bed. "What are you doing up?"

Four and a half years ago, the Mother had blessed them with their first child—a boy, who'd taken Kailevi's heart in his tiny fist and owned him ever since. Which was more than fine; that's what his heart had been made for.

Crouching low, opening the door a little wider, Kailevi smiled at Eaon's bashful fidgeting, bare toes wriggling against the thick rug. He was small for his age, but Ellissa said he was fine; it was common among the Nemuse for their witchlings to wait until ten or eleven to sprout.

Stepping closer, his little fingers reaching for the hem of Kailevi's shirt, Eaon whispered, "There was crying."

"You heard that all the way from your room? You must have very good ears. But don't worry, it was just your sister."

The concept of having a sister had taken a while for Eaon to wrap his head around. They'd gone through all the expected phases: curiosity, then concern and jealousy, but finally excitement. He had talked to Ellissa's swelling belly every day, telling the fetus about all the things he knew—the alphabet, numbers, the different animals that lived at their manor, the sounds they made and the food they liked, as well as all his unts', unks' and cousins' names. He informed her that oranges were the best fruit, but cabbage was to be avoided if at all possible. Quite seriously, he assured Ellissa's bump that, one day, she too would know these things.

"Is she okay?"

"She's fine, she just woke up hungry. Babies cry when they need things because they can't talk yet." Kailevi brushed back Eaon's unruly curls, heart melting at the little frown on his face. "Would you like to come in and see?"

Nodding with his whole body, Eaon followed him back to bed.

Almost every night ended with the four of them crammed on one mattress. There was a crick in Kailevi's neck from Eaon's habit of using his head as a pillow, but it changed nothing—this was happiness.

Crawling into the space between his parents, Eaon calmed at the sight of his sister passing out, drunk on milk.

"See? She's fine."

Nodding again, Eaon made no move to return to his own room. Instead, with absolutely no idea how debilitating it was, he looked up at Kailevi with his big brown eyes, beaming with hope. "Story?"

Ellissa pressed her lips together and closed her eyes, endlessly amused as she moved their daughter onto her shoulder.

"I already told you a story tonight when I put you to bed, remember?" Kailevi chided, though he too was desperately suppressing a smile. "Aren't you too tired?"

"No." Adamant. Pleading. "I'm not. Promise."

Of course not.

"Alright then, just a quick one. Want to hear about the friendly tree that saved a lost sheep again?"

"No. A new one."

"Hmm." Kailevi had gotten in the habit of crafting his adventures into child-friendly tales. Eaon had been happy with the same five over the last six months, asking for them again and again, but it was only a matter of time before his appetite grew. As Ellissa drew out a burp from the baby, pulling her back down to sleep on the cushion of her chest, he had an idea. "Alright. How about the story of an adventurer who crossed the whole world to find a mysterious treasure?"

Eaon's eyes lit up, hands fisting in the sheets. Lying down,

Kailevi made room for his son to curl up beside him. Ellissa leaned against the bedhead, smiling down at them both.

"Sounds exciting," she teased.

"Oh, it is," Kailevi promised.

And it was.

4

CHAPTER ONE

THE TASTE OF GREEN

IT BEGAN LIKE IT ALWAYS DID—WITH A DREAM.

Ever since forming a coven with his sisters, Kailevi Thorne had been having the most vivid dreams. One of his first had been about blue pears, tarter than average but with the added benefit of allowing one to temporarily taste color. Upon waking, Kai still had a mouthful of *indigo* that had ruined his breakfast.

A few days after, he had been working on a way-finding assignment when a distinctly blue fate line caught his attention. That it was the middle of the night was of no consequence; Kailevi had followed the fate line all the way to the docks, arriving in time to witness summer's first crates arriving from Rothvale—among which were those very pears. He had bought one out of curiosity, delighted and terrified when the world around him suddenly developed *flavor*.

"I think green is my favorite," Kailevi told his two sisters later in the academy common room. Olyvia had graduated to tertiary studies last year, Moyra the year before, but they often snuck back into the secondary campus when summoned. "It's . . . fresh, but not like mint. More like . . . "

"Grass?" Olyvia snorted.

Olyvia was the middle child and the biggest paradox Kailevi had ever known. She was somehow both a skeptic and a romantic, bitter and sweet. She mocked his love for the taste of green and in the same breath took a piece of the fruit into her own mouth, eyes lighting from within.

"Oh, Mother above, Kai. Why waste your time looking at green when you could be tasting red?"

"Red? Seriously? Red is garbage."

"You're garbage."

Kailevi leaned across the table to pinch her, but thought better of it when Moyra snapped her fingers.

"Stop it," she warned before returning her attention to the pears. It was late enough that only the most devout to their studies were still using the mahogany desks, faces shadowed by lamplight. The thick velvet drapes blocking the window's views of the sprawling academy outside helped muffle the sound of their secrets. "You say you dreamed of these?"

Moyra was the eldest, sensible and cautious. She did not taste the fruit but prodded at its firm flesh with her pinkie.

"Yes," he said, scowling at Olyvia, who poked out her tongue. "One of your type, I think."

Because before forming a coven with Olyvia and Moyra, before they had pooled their power together into a communal supply, his dreams had been of the average, unremarkable kind. His talents leaned toward way-finding, but whatever latent power in him that yearned for the dreamscape had been amplified by Moyra's own inclinations.

Yet she shook her head. "The dreamscape doesn't work like that. It's a place for the subconscious, not for future-telling.

That's the stars' work. Unless you heard about these pears earlier, or read about them and just forgot, then maybe the dreamscape may have shown them to you, but—"

"Oh, yawn," Olyvia interrupted. "Save the schoolwork for school hours, would you?"

This time Moyra stuck out her tongue, leaned back in her seat, and made a point not to stop Kailevi from picking up one of the school newsletters abandoned on their table, rolling it into a baton, and whacking their sister on the head.

"Ow!"

"Shush." Kailevi teased. "We're trying to have a conversation here."

"Oh, I'm sorry, I didn't realize grass was so important to you."

Moyra sighed and ignored him and Olyvia as they started arguing about the taste of colors again.

He never did figure out how to explain what green tasted like, because color didn't taste the way food or smells did. Green was petrichor. It was lying in a dewy field after a summer rain and breathing the very essence of life deep into your lungs.

His latest dream was full of green.

Perfect fields and rolling hills, broken only by the crystalline waters of a river network winding its way to the edges of green cliffs, the water plummeting so far it misted the valleys below. Even the stones were green with moss and lichen.

And just like the sense of life the pear had left in his mouth as he'd gazed upon what little green there was in Ahrenhale, he was struck paralyzed in his dorm bed by the life force of *her*. Because this night, he had dreamed of a girl. Sun-browned skin and bright honey eyes, she smiled coyly. Her laugh still echoed through his body as she danced in a field of daisies. She looked like green tasted, and he had the sudden urge to paint the world with her and only eat pears for the rest of his life.

Moyra said the dreamscape was a place for the subconscious, but Kailevi had never seen anything like this green girl. Barefoot and wild, there was no space for her in a city like Ahrenhale, and he had never ventured beyond the city's walls.

"Do you think there's latent seer abilities in our bloodline somewhere?" he asked Moyra the next time she visited.

"Why?" she asked in return, because she could never just answer a question.

"More than half my vivid dreams have elicited fate lines that take me to the very thing I dreamed of."

"Do the fate lines appear because you dreamed of a thing, or do you dream of a thing because you sense the fate line?" Moyra barely looked up from her book as she said it, holding the tome in one hand while bringing a teacup to her mouth with the other.

"So, you don't think we have seer leanings," he summarized.

"It's as likely as you manifesting the dreams into existence."

Kailevi raised an eyebrow. "Is that possible?"

Moyra clicked her tongue at him and sipped her tea. "Do you even do your homework?"

"No."

As unhelpful as the conversation had been, it had given Kailevi an idea. If he was dreaming about things on the other end of fate lines that he sensed inherently without seeing, then it was possible the green girl was real. It was possible he could find her.

On weekends, the three Thorne siblings went home. Boarding at the academies wasn't mandatory, but their childhood limestone townhouse in the city's crammed streets had been crowded as children and downright claustrophobic once they reached their teens. There was a nostalgia in returning, though. It was in the attic there where the three of them had bound their blood, magic and souls. It was in their shared bedroom that they had sworn to protect the secret of their coventry with their lives. Unsanctioned, they could all end up in prison. United, they had gotten out of their parents' apothecary.

The stink of alcohol and patchouli emanated a solid six feet from the front door, ensuring Ahrenhale's civilized citizens gave the porch a wide berth. Kailevi had to clamber over the line of sprawled bodies, either sleeping or limp with madness, to reach the bell. He rang it twice, as was custom when he and his sisters came to visit, looking for anything to distract himself from the itching in his nose. The green banner depicting a thread and needle that hung above the door needed re-dying; a job that would get one of them out of the house for a while.

"Dibs," Olyvia barked at the same moment Kailevi opened his mouth to call the same. Scowling, he kicked her ankle. Indignant, she kicked him back.

Moyra rolled her eyes as she hiked up her long skirt, stepping over the legs of a sleeping man. "Both of you are ridiculous."

It took a while, but finally they heard hurried footsteps inside. Moyra frowned a second before the door swung open, and for a moment, Kailevi was too stunned to react. It wasn't their mother or father who opened the door, but a man so thin and dirty he could have passed as a wood nymph. He filled the doorway with his wiry limbs, his wide gaze staring down at the three of them in their uniforms.

When he settled on Olyvia, he sucked in a breath and screamed.

"No! No! Not you! You'll die and ruin us all!"

Then his hands were around her throat. Stumbling under the weight of the man throttling her, Olyvia tripped over the splayed legs of the sleeper behind them and hit the pavement hard. Moyra screamed. Heart in his throat, Kailevi jumped down from the porch and wrapped his arm around the untrained witch's neck.

Before he could pull, though, another arm was around his, wrenching him away and tossing him aside.

"Don't hurt him, it's not his fault!" Levi Thorne scowled at his son before crouching by the rabid witch and gently tugging at his elbow. "Come on, Wade. Let go of her. Let's get you that tonic."

"Papa!" Moyra cried from the porch. "He is killing her!"

The words were barely out before the male fell limp. Olyvia gagged and shoved him off, the constellation on her forehead shimmering urgently. Though Wade no longer appeared to be a threat, Kailevi crawled to his sister and put his body between them, moving her hand from her throat to inspect the damage.

"Can you breathe?"

Olyvia nodded.

Their father didn't pay them any mind, helping the subdued witch to an upright position and checking his vacant eyes. "Damn it, Olyvia, how many times have I told you not to spell-cleave when the untrained are in a frenzy? I won't be able to get his dosage right."

With a glare that could melt the planet's ice caps, Moyra helped Olyvia to her feet first, then offered Kailevi a hand. The three of them left their father on the porch, pushing into the house and immediately up the stairs. Crooked picture frames adorned the walls while herbs hung drying from the railing; practice had them nimbly dodging the piles of books and clothes cluttering the stairs until they reached the second floor.

Their bedroom door was locked tight, but every other room upstairs was filled with witches lost in their minds. The three weren't interested in hiding away in their room though, nor were they interested in answering their mother's call from the bathroom where she was undoubtedly trying to clean someone up. Instead, Kailevi jumped for the rope dangling from the ceiling, pulling on it to bring down a hidden ladder that would take them to the attic.

Clambering up, Moyra pulled the ladder after them and slammed the ceiling door closed.

Peace.

"Are you sure you're alright?" Moyra asked, nervous, inspecting the discolouring around Olyvia's neck.

"I'm okay," she promised, sounding clear enough for it to be true. Wincing, she reached for Kailevi's arm. "Are you?"

Kailevi's shirt had torn at the elbow, scraped bloody. He hadn't even noticed. Sighing, he picked dirt out of the shallow wound. "Yeah. Remind me why we came back here again?"

From farther in the room, a low, silken voice purred. "Because you value your life, little one."

The attic was small, the roof pitched too low to stand upright, and taking up most of the floor space sat three impatient faeries, trapped in a salt circle and staring at their witches longingly.

Stepping inside the ring, Kailevi sat and let his familiar crawl into his lap. Eve was a little thing, a white desert fox no bigger than a regular house cat. Fur soft, tail plush, large ears perked high with excitement—one could be forgiven for mistaking her for a regular animal. Kailevi had, when the critter first began stalking him. It wasn't until he found it curled up on his childhood bed, pale sand *everywhere*, that it dawned on him that Eve was fae.

Though she did not speak, he *felt* intrinsically the sand sprite's promise to guide him as he grew into his power. He was eight at the time. It was late for a familiar to be presenting itself, and unusual for it to do so without the presence of a mature witch to help with the process. Luckily, Kailevi had listened to Moyra recount Gatty's arrival many times, and he'd witnessed Olyvia's claiming in person, so even though both his parents were away at the markets, he knew what to do. Telling the stars that the sprite was *his*, he pricked his finger and gave the faerie a drop of blood. In return, the sprite gave him her name. It clanged soundlessly through his mind, unpronounceable in his simple tongue, and so he chose a shortened version to call her out loud.

They'd been together ever since.

Until now.

The separation was painful for both of them, as it was for his sisters and their own familiars. Olyvia hushed a distraught Pip as the pixie flitted around, squawking indignantly at the blossoming bruises. Pip was well-behaved by pixie standards, a relatively harmless annoyance who ignored Kailevi for the most part. Moyra's familiar, on the other hand, he had never taken a liking to.

All familiars had strengths, but the cat sith was in a sinister league of his own. Of the three, Gatty was the only one who could speak, both aloud and telepathically. He melted in and out of shadows as if he were made of them, and when provoked, could transform into a foul beast. There weren't many witches in Pyxis Academy with familiars of such caliber, and everyone, including the principal, had been shocked when Gatty arrived at Moyra's side.

Kailevi didn't understand it. With coventry pooling their power, the three Thorne siblings ought to be equal, and yet,

Moyra had been singled out as special. The bite of jealousy was an ugly feeling he waved away quickly every time it churned—he adored Eve and wouldn't trade her for anything. Besides, he couldn't begrudge Moyra her status. She very rarely got to be the special one growing up. Olyvia was obnoxious and demanded attention. Kailevi was the only boy. Quiet, serious Moyra was often overlooked, especially by their parents despite being the only one who'd taken an interest in the family's herbology business.

"You are tired," Gatty accused, licking honey off his paw.

Kailevi swallowed his retort—*And the sky is blue; tell me something I don't know*. None of them slept well without the security of their familiars nearby.

His snark may have been silent, but Gatty glared at him and thumped his tail as if he'd heard. Not for the first time, he wondered if the telepathy went both ways.

"Only one more week," Moyra promised. "One more, and Principal Tran will end your banishment."

It wasn't uncommon for familiars to go through bouts of banishment. There's only so much a witch can expect in terms of behavior when you have hundreds of faeries gathered in a single place, and if Gatty and Pip were going to insist on following Moyra and Olyvia back onto the secondary campus, then they would have to endure the same consequences Eve did when they inevitably got into trouble.

"Just in time, too." Kailevi smiled as Eve nuzzled into his throat. "My exams are coming up."

He'd been looking forward to them ever since Olyvia had left Pyxis Academy. Two-thirds of their coven were specializing at the tertiary campus, and the distance was wearing on him. In a couple of weeks, though, he would get his constellation. His eyes would change to reflect his birthstone.

"I am still deeply offended by the accusations to begin with," Gatty bemoaned. "I am no thief."

"You stole Principal Tran's Sol cards," Olyvia reminded him, plucking Pip out of her hair.

Gatty scowled. "I didn't *steal* them. I took them. There's a difference."

"Doesn't matter." Moyra waved a hand, dismissing the argument. "It's nearly over."

One more week, and they could stop visiting their parents' home as regularly. Could care for their familiars' needs without traipsing across the city every weekend.

Standing as best he could, Kailevi tucked his little fox inside his jacket, scratching between her ears as he asked, "You ready for your sunning?"

"An hour," Olyvia reminded, dipping her finger into a pot of honey and letting Pip suckle it off. "Or Tran will know and the banishment will be extended."

"Yes, thank you, Lyv. I am aware."

Of all of them, he was the last who needed to be reminded of the banishment's constraints. Without a constellation, he relied upon his familiar more than the others; his magic was still raw, unrefined, and accessing it took a larger toll. Without training, he'd be lost to it like the witches downstairs. Without Eve, he could easily hurt himself, pushing too hard. Without a constellation tattoo, he couldn't focus it all, and thus would never reach his full potential. Power couldn't be given to those unprepared to harness it, though, hence the exams.

He was ready for it, and with Eve at his side, it wouldn't be long until he was studying beside his sisters once more.

Creeping back down the ladder, he moved silently through the halls, past the closed bathroom door and down the stairs. He could hear his father counseling someone in the living room, so he thought he had a clear shot to the backyard until:

"Kai-kai?"

Cringing, Kailevi froze. His mother must have left the bathroom.

"I know you're there."

Taking a few steps back, he poked his head into the kitchen. As always, there was mess everywhere—piles of used flasks and vials filled the sink, questionable stains seeped into the tiles, the counters covered in chopped herbs. Alcohol and patchouli overwhelmed the lavender and garlic boiling in a pot on the stove, the combination acrid enough to give him a headache.

"Mama."

Frazzled, smudges of burnt herbs covering her face and hands, Kathryn Thorne held out her arms for an expectant hug. "Oh, how I've missed you. Is it the weekend already?"

He couldn't bear to step farther into the room, so he shook his head. "I only have an hour to sun Eve. I'll come back and see you when I'm done."

Disappointed, she dropped her arms. "Papa said you were fighting with the untrained outside."

"Papa almost let one strangle Olyvia to death," he spat, backing down the hallway. "I'll talk to you later."

"Kai."

"Later."

"Can you at least bring back some more rosemary and mint from the yard while you're out there?" she called after him.

Grunting in the affirmative, he nimbly dodged the male lying prone on the floor and made his way outside. There was no structure to the garden, but at least there was fresh air and a little quiet. Every inch of the small yard was intentionally overgrown; the more they could grow themselves the less they had to purchase from vendors, and considering the Thornes didn't charge the untrained for their tonics—let alone board while they recovered from the madness that took them—the family needed to save every penny they could.

Tuition at the academies wasn't cheap.

As frustrated as he was with his parents, Kailevi at least had to thank them for ensuring the three siblings didn't end up languid and untrained in one of the rooms upstairs.

Eve jumped from inside his jacket and immediately began rolling in a sun-baked patch of dirt. Kailevi's grin was short lived as his head gave a sharp throb; they'd been home less than an hour and he already couldn't wait to leave again.

Letting Eve soak, he moved to a bush and plucked a stalk of rosemary.

The sun exploded.

Pain flashed through his skull as the world went white. His skin was hot, blistering, but as quick as it came on, it was soothed by a balm of green. A waft of damp, cool air stole away any lingering discomfort, and then . . .

Her.

Smiling, dancing, skirts billowing as she spun and spun, she held a sunflower to her face and—

Prickling pain pierced his chest. The tangled garden came back into focus. Gasping, Kailevi sat up. He didn't remember falling. Despite Eve sitting on his lap, claws in his chest, he was impossibly cold. His hands shook as he stroked her fur.

"What in the Mother-made world was that?" he wheezed. Though even as he said it, he suspected. Despite what Moyra said, he was having seer visions.

It was less concerning than it should be. The taste of green lingered on his tongue.

CHAPTER TWO

SPELL-CLEAVER

EVE'S CLAWS DIDN'T HELP MUCH THE NEXT TIME MORVIA'S realms clouded his mind. Halfway down the hall to his first exam, his vision grew hazed with fate lines so bright and demanding that he had to stop walking. Lowering himself to the floor, he clung to Eve, trying to stay anchored in his body.

Staying present when Morvia's realms descended wasn't natural, rather a skill he'd spent the entire first month at the academy learning to manage. It took a lot of work to stay focused while his mind and body were pulled in two different directions, his consciousness thrown into a realm of color and mist. When his exams were over and he received his tattoo, the abundance of magic he had access to would be easier to control, but he wouldn't be taught how to wield it beyond basic spells until he could prove he could handle the responsibility of it first.

Of course, being part of a coven amplified everything. He'd learned control a long time ago.

Color in every conceivable shade latticed the world, each indicating the different connections and fates in store for the witches roaming the halls. He was used to the gold linking him to his sisters, the pearlescent line binding him to Eve. Unfamiliar, however, was the new silver one winding around his third finger, an energy pulsing along it unlike anything he'd ever felt. Warm and utterly consuming, the world faded away, inconsequential. There was only this fate line. Only the tug in his chest.

Honestly, it scared him.

Fate was passive. It existed, and the choices people held influence over its direction, nothing more than guides one could follow or ignore. Signposts. Learning to decipher their colors, the relationships they represented, untangling the messy webs to discover the secrets within, was the job of a way-finder. The lines weren't meant to pulse. They weren't meant to demand. They weren't sentient things that screamed at him to *go* with irrefutable urgency.

Blinking, Kailevi got to his feet. It was a terrible time to be distracted, but as the minutes ticked by and he failed to suppress the need to follow the silver thread floating into the distance, he knew there was no point attending his exam. He would fail. He could not see past Morvia's magic right now. Couldn't think.

Eve mewled as he turned back toward his dorm.

"Your tomfoolery has disturbed my sleep."

Kailevi's fists were flying before his eyes were open. They connected with shadow, the creature within rematerializing only after Kailevi had properly woken. Eve barked her high-pitched annoyance, but the only sign that Gatty cared about the sprite's irritation was the narrowing of his moon-bright eyes.

"Library. Now."

"You scared the shit out of me," Kailevi complained, rolling out of bed.

"That doesn't sound like my problem. Every minute you delay my return to bed, however, is yours. Dress quickly."

Biting his tongue, he did as he was told before following the cat sith through the academy halls to the perpetually open library. There were so few students inside that it was easy to spot the two who didn't belong anymore; Moyra and Olyvia had settled at a desk by an open window, hiding their faces in books.

Smothering a yawn, he went to sit beside them.

Moyra slapped her book closed, glaring icily. "What were you thinking?"

"This may come as a surprise, but I think many things," Kailevi snapped back.

Olyvia rolled her eyes and smacked him up the back of the head. "You can't miss your exam and think we won't hear about it. Have you lost your mind?"

"Oh, gods, have you?" Moyra asked, wrath bleeding away as her eyes unfocused, checking his aura.

"No." Kailevi glared at Olyvia as he rubbed the sting from his scalp. "I just . . . I got distracted."

"Distracted." From within the bundle of Olyvia's frizzy brown hair, Pip peeked out and bared her pointy teeth at him. Apparently, nobody was impressed with this late-night visit.

He didn't know how to explain without worrying them, so he braced for it in advance and said plainly, "The fate lines overwhelmed me. One of them was so intense that I couldn't focus on anything else. If I'd gone to my exam, I'd have failed it. At least now I can reschedule."

In every way that Olyvia was loud, Moyra was quiet. In every way his eldest sister was aloof, the other was rowdy. And yet, in that moment, they wore perfectly matching expressions.

It was Moyra who found her voice first. "Has it grown too much for you? Do you need one of Mama's tonics?"

"No, I'm fine," he assured her.

"Don't give us that bullshit," Olyvia warned, pointing a finger. Pip perched on it and pointed at him too. "If you're unraveling, if the pool is overwhelming you—"

"I'm fine, Lyv. I promise. This fate line was just different."

"Kai, you missed your exam," Moyra said, as if he wasn't aware. "Do you not realize how serious this is?"

"You don't understand." Kailevi clenched his fists on the table. Now wasn't the time for them to pull their big-sister crap. "This fate line is brighter than the rest. It's magnetizing. The purest silver I've ever seen. If I didn't know better, I would say Morvia herself is pulling me south."

In fact, that was exactly what he had deduced in the hours cloistered away in his dorm, scrying into a silver mirror.

"Like, to Ewich?" Olyvia wrinkled her nose.

"No." Kailevi lowered his voice to a whisper, despite the two other students in the library being so far away and so absorbed in their work that they likely wouldn't hear him if he shouted. "Like, south of the wards."

Anyone would have thought he'd said something taboo judging by the way Moyra gasped, a hand at her throat. "That's impossible."

He knew that, and yet, it was undeniable. "It's my destiny, Moyra."

"Well." Olyvia tossed her hair over her shoulder. "Looks like you're out of luck. Those wards are solid."

For two thousand years, southern Nir had been isolated from the rest of the world. Thryce Point Bay's surrounding territories kept as much of an eye on what was going on as they could, but the only way to bypass the wards was via moonstone, and those were under strict control of the high council. Fairly enough, too. Once inside, the magic of the wards made it difficult to remember the outside world. Made it difficult to remember why they'd gone in the first place. It was dangerous, in every way a place could be dangerous, and so there was no traveling south without the council's permission. If Kailevi's fate line was important enough to warrant the travel, the high seer would have come to fetch him by now. But they hadn't.

Nobody was going to give him a moonstone, but he didn't think he'd need one. He had a different idea.

Kailevi caught Olyvia's eye and held it. "Maybe."

His sister was incredibly good at what she did. So good, in fact, that she was training under the high spell-cleaver directly. It didn't take long for her to realize what Kailevi was thinking.

"You want me to cleave the wards." As she said it, Olyvia's forehead tattoo began glowing.

"What are you doing?" he hissed.

"Putting a kill order on the magic that lets seers see us right now, lest we all end up in prison just for thinking the idea. Mother forbid."

"Will that work?" whispered Moyra.

Olyvia grimaced and crossed her fingers.

Despite his exhaustion, Kailevi rallied his blessing to peer at the fate lines connecting the three of them. Their bond was as strong as ever, but the lines between them and the rest of the world had gone hazy, bleeding into the atmosphere like ink in water. Nothing seemed out of place, though. Moyra's fate line was thick and strong, even if he couldn't see how far it stretched anymore. Olyvia's was bright and convoluted, as always.

"I don't see any immediate departure, but some weird stuff is going on right now."

Moyra made an offended sound in the back of her throat. "Probably because you're planning on literal treason!"

"Please," Kailevi begged. "You don't know what this feels like. I'll never sleep another night until I find what lies at the other end of this fate line."

"It's insanity!" Moyra argued, but Olyvia had a gleam in her eye that promised trouble.

His heart flipped over twice, hope and desperation rife. It was probably overdramatic, but it truly felt as if he might die if he couldn't go.

Of course, Olyvia's motivations were more complex.

"The council is never going to vote in favor of uniting Nir," she whispered. The three of them were unanimous in their stance regarding the unification of Nir—the people trapped down south had no idea what was brewing within their borders and were criminally underprepared should things go awry—but again, while Moyra wrote persuasive essays to newsletters, Olyvia stormed the streets, protesting loudly. "Maybe it's time we took matters into our own hands."

"No." Moyra shook her head. "No, we're not messing with the wards. I won't be a part of this."

A righteous anger burned deep in Kailevi's belly, but Moyra didn't shy from it. Never had. She had always been the water to his and Olyvia's fire, but he was eighteen now; she was not the boss of him anymore.

Before he could say as much, Olyvia caught his eye. She, too, wasn't interested in following orders anymore.

Shrugging, Olyvia said, "Stay here then."

Under the table, Gatty growled. Moyra's face dropped.

It hurt, not just his sister but his own heart too. Once upon a time he'd been sure there was nothing that could fracture their coven; if he could ignore Morvia's call, he would, but even considering it intensified the fate line's draw. He wasn't a strong enough witch to defy the will of a High Spirit. Especially not one infamous for their indifference.

"I need to do this," he begged her to understand. "I can feel it."

Further arguing was pointless. Leaving their eldest sister spluttering, Olyvia and Kailevi stood. They needed to make a plan.

"Olyvia, stop!" Moyra shouted.

Olyvia didn't stop.

"Kailevi, listen to me!"

He couldn't.

"Are you sure you can't wait until after your exams at least? You need your constellation."

In the privacy of Kailevi's dorm, Olyvia flopped onto the narrow bed against the wall and voiced the scrap of doubt she'd never show in front of Moyra.

Shoving clothes and books into the largest pack he was capable of carrying, Kailevi shook his head. "With how fiercely it's pulling me, I don't think I'd pass my exams anyway. I can't think past it. I have to do this, Lyv. I have to do it now. I'll figure it out, and if it gets too much, I'll come back. And I'll have Eve."

The sand sprite was lazing in the window, belly up, eyes closed, while Pip, apparently no longer tired, was using the soft fur of Eve's underside as a trampoline, sending grains of sand bouncing all over the desk.

"Maybe . . ." Olyvia hesitated, as if she hadn't finished thinking the thought before speaking. "Maybe I'll come with you?"

Every muscle in his body froze. "Lyv."

"Kai."

"*Lyv.*"

"Kai-kai."

Leaving his travel bag for a moment, he grabbed his pillow from the bed and made to whack her with it. As soon as it was in his hands, though, Olyvia sat up and batted it away.

"Rude."

"Do not call me that," he warned, lifting the pillow over his head in a clear threat.

Olyvia just laughed at him. "Or what? You'll go crying to Moyra?"

The laughter died as they both remembered the way their sister had begged. Kailevi put his pillow down and went back to his bag. "You can't leave her too."

"Why not?" she argued, throwing her hands up. "She might be content to sit around here doing the bare minimum but I'm not. If I went south with you, I could actually help the people stuck in there instead of just arguing in circles about it up here."

"Well, if not for Moyra, then you should stay because you're literally training under the high spell-cleaver. In a few decades, you could be taking over his position. You could do way more for the south as a councillor."

Olyvia sighed and flopped back down, her pixie abandoning its trampoline and flitting to nest in her hair again. Pip squared for a bit and Olyvia listened intently, as if she understood. She heaved another great sigh before declaring, "I'll figure it out by the time we get there. I'll bring a bag, just in case. Meet me at the southern bridge in two hours?"

He wanted to argue more but he loathed becoming a hypocrite. Olyvia was going to do whatever she wanted, his opinion on the matter be damned.

"At least leave Moyra a note, would you?" he called as Olyvia got off the bed and pushed open the dorm's window. "Let her know your plans. Let her know she can meet us if she changes her mind."

With a wink, his sister slipped over the ledge and out of sight.

The last thing Kailevi managed to squeeze into his pack was a box, inside which he kept his fragile possessions—a few crystals, a glass orb, and the last blue pear he'd gotten his hands on before the vendor sold out. He'd preserved the flesh in a jar, meaning to savor it for as long as he could.

The hair on the back of his arms stood on end a moment before the shadows beneath his bed began to twist.

"You've upset your sister." Gatty's tone woke Eve, who slipped from the desk to sit on Kailevi's feet.

"Some things are more important than Moyra's feelings," Kailevi answered, shrugging into a jacket before lacing his boots. "If the situation was reversed, if she had a dream about something as important as this fate line feels, she'd be doing the exact same thing."

It took until Kailevi had shouldered his pack, tucked Eve into his jacket pocket and assessed the drop to the lawn from his window for Gatty to respond.

"You are not incorrect."

Kailevi choked on a scoff. That was not what he expected Gatty to say, but then again, he was no expert on faerie loyalty. He did know enough lore not to walk away, though; it was rude to turn your back on a faerie, and poor etiquette could cost a lot. So he waited, folding his arms over his chest impatiently.

Waited. For thirty whole seconds, he waited before realizing Gatty was waiting for him.

Settling against the windowsill, Kailevi considered what he

wanted to say. Considered, given the likelihood that he'd never see the cat sith again, what needed to be addressed.

"I know you and I got off on the wrong foot," he began.

Gatty bared his fangs. "You are trouble, and I dislike Moyra's proximity to trouble."

"I also know," Kailevi went on, "that familiars usually leave their witches once they no longer need guidance. Moyra is nearly fully trained, but . . . I'll give you something, if you promise to take care of her while we're gone."

Dangerous words spoken to a dangerous fae.

"So brash," Gatty chided, offended. "As long as your soul is bound to my witch, making an offer like that, to any fae, will be a death sentence I enjoy carrying out. Alas, you need not offer me anything. Despite her training, I don't believe she will be ready for independence for a very long time. Where she goes, I will follow."

That was one anxiety relieved, at least.

"Then, I apologize for upsetting her."

"Noted," Gatty purred, form melting into the shadows once again. "I do hope you find what you're looking for. I have an inkling you're correct about Morvia's meddling."

A terrifying thought.

The bustling towns spattered along the desert roads were highly distracting with their markets and fairs, their taverns and divination huts; only the urgent pulsing of the fate line kept Kailevi moving. Neither he nor Olyvia had ever crossed the gem-studded bridge out of Ahrenhale—they'd heard stories of what it was like, but experiencing it was entirely different.

Lively and budding with trade, the people friendly and

generous, it wasn't difficult to find someone willing to give them a ride to the next town over in exchange for a copper coin. The next one had fewer Morvish witches living there, and so they were able to bargain another ride in exchange for a few palm readings. It was easy work, and traveling by horse cut the time it took to reach the divide between northern and southern Nir by half. Sticking to the eastern coast would have been an even faster journey, but the fate line pulled them inland, and Kailevi was not willing to risk deviating from Morvia's insistence.

The last leg was made on foot, and when they eventually reached their destination, exhausted and sunburnt, the wonders of the desert towns were forgotten.

Until this moment, Kailevi hadn't truly understood the meaning of the word "mountainous."

Daylight crested over cloud-brushing peaks, the range stretching from the dormant volcano marking Qiri's western border all the way to the eastern coast. Shrubbery couldn't grow this deep in the desert, the harsh slope of the mountain walls a barren and merciless barrier. When Kailevi unfocused his eyes, he could see the tangle of fate lines butting against the invisible wards where only a few were able to push through.

Olyvia looked at the boundary as a starving man might look at a feast.

Spell-cleaving was an underrated affinity. Seers struggled to see her, star-readers complained of the sky's silence whenever she was near; with minimal effort, Olyvia could render every witch in her presence useless. Her reputation recently brought Councilor Pearl to visit the academy, and in true Ahrenhalian style, gossip ran rife about Pearl's feud with the high spell-cleaver. She wanted Olyvia for herself, to train as Qiri's next emissary to the Sparrow Coven. The rate with which emissaries lost contact with the council had everyone on edge, given they'd gone to a city inhabited by witches devoted to the High Spirit of Death. But a spell-cleaver would be safe from hexes and curses. A well-trained one would be untouchable.

"Can you feel it?" she asked.

Their coventry meant that Kailevi's own ability to sense wards had amplified beyond his natural inclination, but was still far less powerful than his sisters.

"A little."

"There is nothing in the world like it," she said, breathless. "The power it would take to make something like this, to cast it around such a huge expanse of land . . . It's unfathomable."

Nervously, Kailevi watched Olyvia bounce on the balls of her feet. "Are you sure you can do this? I don't want you to hurt yourself."

"I don't think I could bring it all down." At Pip's squawking, she corrected, "I definitely can't bring the whole thing down, but, I'm fairly sure I can crack it enough for you to slip through."

"Still . . ."

"Kai." Tearing her gaze away from the mountains, her hunger for a challenge gave way to something more doting. "I can't see fate lines as well as you can, but even I can tell that you have to go. You *have* to. I have snacks and tea in my bag in case this gets a bit intense, but we're doing it."

Putting his pack down, he looked up at the mountains and shook his head. The volcano ensured nothing grew on the western side of the range, the dunes hiding the nearby bay so that, from where Kailevi stood, the world seemed dead and barren, yet with the sunrise painting the sand orange and lilac, it was still beautiful. The absence of people, of life, in a paradoxical way, made him appreciate the breath in his body even more. He hadn't understood how big a mountain really was. Hadn't understood how big the world was.

His next breath shook on the way out.

Olyvia put a hand on his shoulder and squeezed, a soft smile dimpling her cheek. "Stop being such a baby."

"Oh, Lover take me, you are the *worst*."

Her cackling broke the last of the tension riding Kailevi's shoulders and a soft vacuum began to pull at his soul as Olyvia began to draw on their communal pool of power. Only complete and utter trust kept him from panicking—Olyvia would not take so much as to kill him.

Coventry was such a careful balance of give and take. Ambition too often led a witch to pool their blessing, just to tug it all back and leave the other two husks. Hence why coventry was so heavily regulated, and why the Thorne siblings would be in terrible trouble if anyone found out what they'd done.

Dropping to her knees, Olyvia threw back her head, lips moving in silent prayer as the constellation on her forehead began to twinkle. Joining her in the sand, Kailevi tucked Eve against his side and braced against the nerves fluttering in his stomach. Slowly, Olyvia's hands rose in an arch until her arms stretched high overhead, reaching for the dawn moon, palms coming together to form a spear. The muttering stopped, every muscle in Olyvia's body tensed, and Kailevi marveled at the strength and speed with which she whipped herself forward, carving her arms through the air.

The universe cracked.

The sound of it reverberated deep in Kailevi's bones, a thunder that shook his insides, ripping apart the essence of his body and mind. Sand and dust exploded in a cloud around them as Olyvia's hands cut into the ground, the mountain trembling in her wake.

It hurt. As if he could feel the mountain's agony in his own body, Olyvia carving through him, ripping him apart, a scream of blinding agony boiled the blood in his veins.

When it was over, all the magic Olyvia had pulled into herself flooded back with a force that sent Kailevi crumpling.

It took a few minutes for his soul to settle again. Nausea burned the back of his throat as he blinked grains of sand out of his eyes, pushing himself upright once more. The dust was landing, the mountain stilling.

Olyvia remained folded over, hands buried in the sand.

Eve shivered. Pip was wailing.

"Lyv," Kailevi croaked, crawling the short distance to where his sister sat limp. "Lyv, are you alright?"

She didn't answer. She didn't move.

Cursing, Kai ripped open her backpack and pulled out a glass bottle of ginseng tea, gently pulling at Olyvia's shoulder to make her sit up. She didn't. Instead, his touch sent her collapsing to the side.

"Shit. Lyv, come on."

Her eyes were closed, lips slack as he uncorked the bottle and tipped the tea against them. Not that ginseng tea was a miracle cure that was going to rouse her from unconsciousness, but still, it should help. Brown liquid spilled down her chin. Fingers against her throat, he felt for her pulse.

He couldn't find it.

"Get it together," he hissed at himself, shaking out his hands and trying again. The adrenaline crashing through his body was making it impossible. "Alright. Alright."

Gently, Eve nuzzled against his leg.

"She'll be fine," Kailevi said, sliding his pack on and lifting his listless sister into his arms. "Just have to get her some help. Come on."

Slogging through the sand, he carried Olyvia to the crack in the mountainside that hadn't been there a few minutes ago. Eve dove in and out of the sand like a selkie in the waves, keeping pace, but when he looked back, Pip was not following.

"Come on!" Kailevi shouted.

The pixie stayed hovering a few inches off the ground where Olyvia's collapsed form had left a divot in the sand.

"Pip, this is not the time for your bratting! Let's go!"

Every minute he stood there screaming at the pixie was a minute his sister didn't have. Kailevi refused to think about why Olyvia's familiar wouldn't come. Even as his vision swam, he told himself they were tears of frustration. Nothing to do with the splitting pain in his heart and soul.

"I will fucking leave you!" he cried one last time.

Pip resumed her mournful wailing, a somber song that followed him into the dark.

CHAPTER THREE

A SPARROW'S CURSE

IT WAS ALARMING TO REALIZE HE WAS WAKING UP. HE DIDN'T remember going to sleep. Falling unconscious? He didn't remember what happened, only that it must have been terrible if coming awake was to be such a torturous affair. From the spot between his brows to the very top of his crown, his skull throbbed. His eyelids were sandpaper, yet he managed to open them.

Doing so explained nothing.

It was dark, but not night-dark, and not absolutely. There was a hole in the rock-hewn wall with a naked flame sitting within, uncontained and fueled by nothing.

The fire smiled at him.

It was so strange that Kailevi was sure his mind had unraveled, except that, for once, his thoughts were exceptionally clear. Quiet. His blessing hadn't been this settled since before he'd made coventry, and the world outside his mind seemed louder for it. Not that there was much to hear, the loudest being

32

footsteps echoing somewhere far from the little room he lounged in.

The fire winked, its giggle a crackle. Kailevi blinked at the little flame in its divot, waiting for it to start making sense, but it continued to laugh at him for longer than a lapse in sanity should allow.

If it was real, understanding his surroundings was paramount. Flickering firelight bounced off the walls in a muted rainbow, reflecting off colorful glass mosaiced into the stone. The ceiling and the floor were made of stone, too—No. Not *made* of stone, the way the floors at his parents' house were made of wood. Something about the air, the weight of it, the way sound traveled . . . The stone existed first, and a room, a home, had been carved into it.

Without mercy, it came back to him in a deluge of pain.

The desert.

The mountains.

The wards.

Throwing back a thick fur blanket, he clambered up from a pile of oversized cushions and held onto the wall until his head stopped spinning.

"Lyv?" he called, knowing full well that she wouldn't answer. The tether that bound him to his sister had broken. He could not feel her anymore.

His ribs were raw with the pain of it, and no matter how he pressed on the bones, he couldn't relieve it. Desperate, he reached for the other bond that stretched farther than it ever had before. Moyra was alive. And she would know, as he did, that Olyvia was not.

"Eve?" Another tether, taut as ever. A grumble among the pile of cushions, followed by a pale snout sticking out from within the folds of furs. His familiar yawned, her lack of concern an assurance that he was safe.

He'd trade his safety for his sister's in a heartbeat.

"What happened?" he asked aloud, though nobody was there to answer him. Sliding to the floor, he brought up his knees and rested his pounding head on them.

Distantly, he could feel the sticky remnants of a salve on his skin, but when he looked, there was only pinked flesh to show for whatever wounds he'd earned. Jagged rock, he recalled. Pressing in on all sides. He'd been squeezing through a too-narrow crack in the mountain, trying to keep Olyvia from scraping against the rough stone, tearing his own skin bloody in the process. Kailevi remembered his panic. There wasn't enough air. Surrounded by mountain, the walls squeezed him too tight.

Then the air had changed, charged with static energy. The barest whisp of warding touched his skin; Olyvia hadn't cleaved all the way through. As thin and fragile as it was, he thought he could push through—and he'd been right, but by the Mother, her Lover and their sacred Balance had it burned.

Eve tried to help, barking furiously, small pulses of power bursting against the malevolent veil of magic, but it wasn't enough, and between the panic and the pain, he'd started screaming.

He must have lost consciousness.

So, how did he get here?

Eve's snuffling made him lift his head. The sand sprite had padded over to a small cabinet hidden in the shadowed corner. Rolling his neck, trying to loosen the taut muscles there, Kailevi crawled over and found a pitcher of water inside.

He'd barely taken a sip when the room brightened, a flap of tapestry pulled back in lieu of a door. Wincing against the pinch in his temples, Kailevi stood quickly, back to the wall and fists curled.

The figure filling the doorway stilled, made a surprised noise, and immediately began babbling in a language Kailevi didn't know.

He couldn't bear to do it for long, but Kailevi unfocused his eyes to glimpse their aura, surprised to find the colors unthreatening. Eve, sitting on his feet, relaxed slightly as Kailevi did.

When the stranger stopped talking and the silence lingered, he realized it was probably his cue to talk. "I don't understand you."

The stranger tilted his head, shaking it slightly. Muttered something else.

Kailevi wasn't fluent in Nirnish as he had, until now, never needed to communicate with anyone outside Ahrenhale. He was also mildly conflicted on how offensive it was that Nirnish had become the common language—human's weren't stupid, they could learn other languages too, but alas, at some point in history witches had decided humans were too simple to be multilingual.

"Do you speak Nirnish?" he tried, cringing at the way his accent butchered the words.

The stranger left.

So, no.

He drank more water, but with every sip he became more hollow. Where was Olyvia's body? What was he going to do with it? The tapestry pulled back again and a smaller figure stepped inside. A female with thick black hair.

"Nirnish?" she asked.

"Yes. You speak it?"

"A little," she answered. "What is your name?"

"Kailevi." He was fairly certain she was not fae—Eve was calm. "Who are you? Where am I? Where's . . . Where's my sister?"

In the flickering light, the woman's eyes were so very kind.

"We've put her somewhere safe. I can take you. My name is Kerrina. You're in the Long Gorge. The Northern Mountain Clan. Brach has questions. How you got inside the mountain, under the temple. What clan are you?"

Long Gorge.

Northern Mountain Clan.

He filed the terms away, unsure what a clan was. Unsure of anything.

"Qiri," Kailevi said, hoping that the magic enclosing southern Nir wasn't so powerful the people inside had forgotten about the small northern territory sea-locked on the other side of the mountains.

Recognition lit Kerrina's eyes. She held out a hand. "Ah. Then come, Kailevi of Qiri. And welcome to Vertlyn."

There wasn't a house built inside the mountain. There was a city.

Fire sprites and globes of eternally burning flame lit the way as Kailevi was led through a maze of tunnels—streets—hundreds upon hundreds of homes branching off. Colored glass and gem fragments were laid in patterns, a mosaic beneath his boots, while tapestries and blackened metal frames decorated the walls.

The farther along the city he traveled, the more apparent it became that the people here did not believe in shoes. As the tunnel opened into a large underground cavern, rope ladders the only way down to the cavern floor, he watched with awe the ease with which Kerrina clambered down. His boots ensured his descent was far less elegant.

Stepping outside was shocking enough to almost warm the chill Olyvia's absence left in his soul. Apparently Kailevi had seriously underestimated the magnitude of the mountain range —the Long Gorge was a literal name for the place the Northern Mountain Clan had settled. The peaks rose high enough to touch clouds, and all the way up, the sides were threaded with paths and tunnel openings as thousands of witches got on with their day. The sheer rock face also dipped far lower than ground level. So low, in fact, that all there was to see down there was a pool of darkness, speckled with the occasional twinkling . . . star? Were there stars down there?

Kerrina didn't stop to explain. Leading him along a pathway, she ignored the muttering and stares they received. Kailevi tried to rally his blessing again, headache be damned, but something wasn't right. The fate lines were hazy, as they'd been when Olyvia hid them.

Shaking his head, hiding his shaking hands in his pockets, he let the magic fall away.

It took over an hour for them to reach what was undoubtedly the temple Kerrina had mentioned earlier. Isolated from the rest of the city, the air was more sulphurous, the ground warmer, and the tall entrance in the mountain wall had been decorated with far more care and considerably more gemstones than anywhere else.

Two males stood guard, pale brown leather wrapping their severe bodies, spears in hand, bows and quivers on their backs. Two more stood nearby, one with white paint streaking his tanned face, the other with scaled shoulder pads and a twisted circlet of twigs and gold.

"Brach," Kerrina called, and the painted male turned.

The two had a hushed conversation in their own language while Kailevi stood to the side, trying and failing to ignore the way the second male was staring. At his feet, Eve's tail had bristled, but she wasn't growling yet.

"Kailevi." Brach put a hand out to guide Kerrina behind him. "You are from Qiri?"

"Yes. Is my sister here?"

The three mountain witches shared a look.

"Yes," Brach finally answered. "This temple is where the dead are laid to rest. It is where I heard your screaming. Getting you out of that crevice was no easy task. What were you doing in there?"

It occurred to Kailevi at this point that he had been rather reckless, bullying his way into southern Nir with no plan and no idea what to expect. It was stupid to have thought he'd get through the wards and run into nobody, following the silver fate line all the way to his green girl without issue.

"I'm looking for someone," he answered truthfully. "Morvia guided me south of the wards."

Only after he said it did he realize that southern witches might not know about the wards. How was he going to explain?

"Ah," Brach said, derision rife. "The snobbish Morvia and her elitist Qirians are showing an interest in something outside their little bubble."

Blinking, Kailevi had no idea what he was talking about. He should probably be offended, should probably explain more, but . . . But his sister was dead. Olyvia was inside that temple, and all he wanted was to see her.

Kerrina looked like she was going to argue on Kailevi's behalf, smacking Brach with the back of her hand, but before she could say anything, the other male cleared his throat. Authority oozed off him, and both Kerrina and Brach went silent.

"Show me your neck."

Kailevi frowned, but tilted up his chin. With his throat exposed, Eve finally gave into a growl, and all three clan witches took a step back.

"The fae creature won't leave him," Kerrina warned, rubbing the meat of her palm where the skin was slightly pinker than the rest. "Trust me, don't try to get rid of it."

Brach and the other male chose to believe her.

"The back of your neck," the crowned male clarified.

It was a strange request, but he couldn't see how it would hurt. Turning, he lifted the curls off his nape and waited.

A huff. "Not demi-kin. I'm inclined to believe him, then."

Demi-kin. Kailevi added the term to his list of things to figure out later.

"This is what will happen," the male continued. "You may spend what time you need in the temple, then you will leave the gorge."

Before Kailevi could process the command, Kerrina gasped.

"Priest, you cannot send him alone. He is a child, and unfamiliar with the land. He'll be killed."

The crowned priest stared at her, a lone eyebrow lifted, but after a minute of Kerrina's scalding gaze, he heaved an exasperated sigh. "Who is it you are looking for, witchling?"

"I . . ." Sweat beaded down Kailevi's neck, his irritation growing with every exchange. He was not a child. He was eighteen. "I'm not actually sure. I saw her face in a dream."

All three witches shared another look, profound with understanding.

"I see," the priest said.

"What did she look like?" Kerrina asked with a smile.

Sighing, Kailevi rubbed his forehead. His chest was so, so empty, and he was exhausted by their condescension. Petulance wasn't going to get him anywhere, though, and deep down he knew he couldn't let his sister's sacrifice be for nothing. If these witches were willing to help him, he had to let them.

"Green?" That wouldn't mean much to them. "Tanned? She wore this white, gauzy skirt. Mousy hair, curly. I think she likes sunflowers."

The priest snorted, but Brach was nodding. "Anfar Forest Clan, for sure."

Kailevi filed the name away.

"Definitely," the priest agreed, avoiding Kerrina's pleading gaze. It must have elicited the desired effect anyway because he let loose another weary sigh. "Alright. *Alright*. This is what we'll do. Some of our people are heading to Anfar for a trading festival in a few days. There's safety in numbers; you may travel with them. But we keep your Qirian status a secret. It does not leave this circle. If word spreads, we'll have Sparrows on our ass in minutes."

It was more than he expected. More than he'd thought he'd need. Southern Nir was a cauldron of pending disaster and he truly had not considered how he was going to navigate it. The pull in his chest had made him stupid.

"Thank you."

"Brach!" Brach called.

There was movement from within the shadows of the temple's entrance, but the guards didn't flinch as a small boy came running out with Kailevi's pack. Brach's son, most likely. Named after himself. Kailevi couldn't judge—he too had his father's name.

"Thank you," Kailevi repeated, taking his pack from the boy, who promptly ran to hide behind his father's legs.

Kerrina took Kailevi's arm, smiling pityingly. "Come, sweet."

She guided him inside the temple, and since he had a few

days' grace to process everything, Kailevi let every step into its depths sink him deeper into grief.

~

The Northern Mountain Clan were not witches the way he knew them.

Kailevi had been raised to respect nature, raised in the knowledge of how to use its offerings to heal both body and mind, but he had never been at one with it like these witches were. The way they scaled the mountainside without leaving a trace, even carting wagons and barrels of wares, was remarkable. Gravel crunched beneath his boots, his movement tumbling small rocks down the harsh edge of the path, while the only proof the mountain witches had passed through were the tracks of the wheels, quickly gone as bare feet touched the earth behind them.

When the caravan reached the scraggly bushland at the bottom, it was much the same. The spindly shrubbery grew thicker as they pushed through, the trees thin and white with silvery green leaves, and Kailevi felt like a bull in a ceramic store compared to the clan's grace. Walking with them was intensely spiritual in a way he hadn't experienced before. Physically, he wasn't far from Qiri, yet Vertlyn was worlds away.

It was a few days before they emerged from the bushland into a sprawling field, and Kailevi gave up counting the number of things he'd never seen before. There was no land like this outside the wards, open and vibrant and healthy. Qiri had its own beauty, from its white deserts and crowded cities to turquoise beaches and green lakes where the fernery was thick and smothering in the humidity. But nothing like this. As far as the eye could see, a plain of heather glowed gold and lavender under the bright sun, stalks waving softly in the breeze.

The senior guardian began shouting in a language Kailevi now knew was called Terranian, the tongue of those blessed by the nature spirit Terra.

Brach translated. "We're camping here for the night. A few more days and we will reach the Heart Lake. It's very dangerous. Everyone must be well rested and alert."

"What's dangerous about it?" Kailevi asked as he took off his pack, massaging his aching shoulders.

"The Vein is a river that runs from the Northern Spine to the eastern ocean, and there are only two places it can be crossed—a bridge near the city of Pirevia, which should be avoided at all costs, and another bridge near the Heart Lake on the western side. The fae know this. Beasts, too."

Brach looked to where Eve was pawing at the earth, sand falling from her fur to make a soft bed to rest in.

"People don't seem to like the fae much, here," Kailevi noted.

Brach was what the clan called a "scout," and he was already surveying the nearby area, prodding at the ground looking for a spot to pitch a tent. "Is it different in Qiri?"

"I mean, we're not stupid—nobody trusts the fae. But we understand them. We coexist. They're a part of life."

"Hm." Brach passed Kailevi a ball of twine to start binding long wooden poles together, as he had done every night they stopped to camp. Kailevi missed his bed. "Here, the fae are important for the land, but they are tricky, selfish, and troublesome. If they can take something from you, they will. If they can use you, they will. Kidnap, enslave, torment—they do what they want. All we can do is try to protect ourselves. But if I had to choose between the fae and the beasts, I would rather face the fae. Better odds of walking away with your life."

"I don't know that we have many beasts in Qiri." Or outside the wards at all. "What is the difference?"

Brach arranged the poles Kailevi had tied and draped a leather blanket over it to create a shelter. "Beasts give nothing to the land. There's no bargaining or reasoning with them, no rules or games. All they do is kill."

"Is a bear a beast?"

"A bear may kill to protect itself, or to eat. A harpy will gut you for the thrill of it. A shtryg will kill you simply because it can. It enjoys your fear."

Kailevi took his waterskin from his pack, adjusting to the new level of danger he was going to be spending his days in. "And they're concentrated at the Heart Lake."

Brach grimaced. "They know the best places to hunt."

If he'd thought the clan was silent before, he learned a new meaning for the word as they crept onto the wood-and-silver bridge crossing the Vein. Unwilling to risk his footfalls, Kailevi had been instructed to hang onto the back of a wagon while the mountain witches lay lengths of wool beneath the wheels, dragging them over the creaky bridge inch by agonizing inch.

Both Eve and Kailevi didn't mind taking a break from walking. The sand sprite lounged across his sweaty neck like a scarf, sunning herself, unconcerned with how her body heat roasted him alive. Between that and his feet, sweltering and blistered, he'd almost sobbed with relief at being told to climb on the wagon. Every muscle from his toes to his glutes burned. He wasn't unfit, but he had also never traversed uneven countryside for a week straight while running on whatever dregs of sleep he could get between nightmares.

He also didn't mind the view.

The mountain's melting ice caps fed the Vein, crashing furiously all the way to the Heart Lake. Clear as glass, the body of water glittered unnaturally under summer's sun, refracting the light against a city of diamond far below the surface. A brave adventurer might take a rowboat out to chip off a piece, except the clarity of the water meant Kailevi could also see the things that lurked among the spires.

Nymphs and selkies were by far the worst things inhabiting the waters in Qiri, but the only one he'd ever seen in person was a familiar who'd followed their witch to the academies all the way from the coast. The creatures peeking out from the waves with their seaweed hair and vicious grins, watching the caravan's procession, weren't anything like it. Their auras were a dark, swirling red that writhed with feral hunger. Worse still was the nokk creeping below the bridge, keeping pace, incandescent eyes unblinking.

A shiver ran down Kailevi's spine, gooseflesh rising. He looked to Brach, who kept an arrow nocked as he inched along. Brach must have felt Kailevi's gaze, because when he caught his eye, he hopped silently up beside him.

So quiet it was barely a breath, Kailevi whispered, "When you return to the Long Gorge, I need you to do something for me."

"What?" Brach asked, dark eyes scanning the water.

"There's a small chance my other sister may come looking for me. Can you keep an eye on the crack in the temple? And if she does emerge, don't let her come this way on her own."

For a long minute, Brach was silent. "Is it very likely that other Morvish witches may come through the crack?"

Truly, Kailevi didn't know. He had no idea what effect Olyvia's spell-cleaving might have had on the Morvish, but, if the spell had been felt through the realms, he strongly suspected other Unifiers may come looking.

"There are some in Qiri," Kailevi said, so very, very softly, "who believe we should be reunited with the rest of Nir. There's a . . . How do I explain this? A prediction, a fate line, suggesting that our world could be threatened by something growing here. The Unifiers want to be part of the fight, if it ever comes to pass."

Brach nodded slowly, brows pinched tight as he fell deep into thought. He still hadn't answered Kailevi by the time the last wagon crossed the bridge, the clan relaxing infinitesimally once back on solid ground.

A loud whistle shattered all relief.

Brach hauled Kailevi off the wagon as the horses pulling it went racing for the nearest tree line, saving him from what would have been a nasty fall. Before he could thank him, though, Brach was throwing him on the ground.

Barking her displeasure, Eve growled and lunged for Brach's ankle, but the mountain witch caught her by the scruff and shoved her into Kailevi's flailing arms.

"Hush!" Brach hissed, yanking at Kailevi's boots and flinging them into the river.

"What—"

Brach smacked a hand over Kailevi's mouth. Eve bit his wrist, but aside from an annoyed hiss, Brach ignored the wound in favor of dragging them both into a dense bush. The rest of the clan had disappeared. The wagons were gone.

Heart beating so violently he could feel it in his temples, Kailevi clutched a squirming Eve to his chest and waited.

A horn blew, followed by a sound Kailevi didn't understand. Not until he saw the dozen soldiers barreling out of the tree line, hollering a battle cry, racing straight for them with silver swords raised high.

Brach's grip on his arm was the only thing that kept Kailevi from running.

Lucky, too. The soldiers weren't attacking the clan; it took a second longer than it should've to notice the half dozen creatures they were chasing.

Kailevi's stomach churned.

Mother knew he hated rats, and these ones were knee high and muscled like small bears. Their tails lashed behind them with such power that, when one caught a soldier in the knees, the man went sprawling, the crack of his bones echoing through the clearing.

The giant rats were making a run for the riverbed, but as they broke from the trees the creatures seemed to realize they weren't going to make it in time. They turned, and Kailevi covered his mouth to keep from vomiting as both man and monster fell victim to bloodshed.

It was quite possible that, even outnumbered, the rats might have won had they not grown distracted by their kill and stopped to gorge themselves.

Brach didn't let go once the battle was over, though. After the surviving men called out that the area was clear, another three dozen people on horses came stalking through the trees. Many wore armor, but there were a few among them in large, lacy dresses or well-fitted, high-collared doublets. One in particular caught Kailevi's attention.

A male sat tall on the back of the largest horse, a crown of golden feathers on his silver head. It was a stark contrast to the black doublet he wore, but the tips of his pointed boots were also dipped in gold, glinting under the sun. Unlike the mountain clan, he was not hiding. He smirked at the corpses bloodying the ground and began calling orders, loud and demanding in a language that was not Nirnish and not Terranian.

"Prince Nevan," Brach breathed in his ear. "Only child of the Sparrow king and queen. They gave him Pirevia as a quarter-century gift and a reward for his successful Passing rite. The river will be red within a century, I guarantee it."

Using meditative breathing, Kailevi forced his body to stay still. To stay calm. The Ahrenhalian public weren't privy to details regarding what passed as authority here in southern Nir, but gossip was a favored currency among the fae, and so word had spread about the false coven who worshipped Death. Kailevi knew that their ideology was based on Balance, but that in practice, they were little more than vicious colonizers.

Nevan's aura was blood red, muted by shadows and pulsing furiously.

In all his life, Kailevi had never feared a fate line, but as he rallied his blessing he was nothing short of nauseous. The lines were still blurred, but he could at least identify them; twisted and tied up with a dozen others, it was difficult to tell much beyond the fact that Prince Nevan had an important role in the fates of many, his influence reaching far.

Seconds later, he forgot about Nevan.

A shining fate line of bright purple interlaced with gold and silver weaved between Nevan, Kailevi, and a witch standing to the side of Nevan's horse. The breath in Kailevi's body was stuck halfway to his lungs as he noted the pattern of her constellation tattoo.

The robust woman had her wrists and ankles shackled, the chain between them only just long enough to let her walk. A rope had been tied around her neck, the other end to the saddle of Nevan's horse. Clearly she was a prisoner. A prisoner of the prince of the Sparrow Coven. It was *outrageous*. If the council knew, they would stop sending new emissaries and start sending assassins. The priest's warning to keep his Morvish status a secret echoed through his head, bile coating his tongue.

Brach's grip tightened. Eve had gone still.

The fate line seemed to originate from her, tying the three of them together, branching off into hazy uncertainty. It was thin, too—something that wouldn't play out for a very long time—but before he could push for clarity, the Morvish witch's gaze snapped right to his.

He stopped breathing. He swore his heart stopped beating.

The witch's wrinkles grew as she smiled, genuinely pleased. Again, it took longer than it should have for Kailevi to pinpoint what it was about the expression that disturbed him.

Once a witch reached biological maturity, their physical aging slowed to such a degree that one could live for hundreds of years and barely change. It was partly due to the diluted relation between fae and witch, and partly Mother's design—she wanted her gifts to the Lover to be perfect, so decay was something witches only did once they arrived in the after realm. Humans were different. They weren't made for the Lover, they were made as prey.

Yet, this Morvish witch had deep wrinkles and a pronounced age spot beneath her left eye. It shouldn't be possible.

Her constellation tattoo shimmered, but whatever she intended never manifested. The dark shadows beneath her eyes deepened, her hair losing more of its luster. Before his very eyes, she aged as a human would given a decade.

Decay was Death's domain.

The Morvish witch had been cursed by a Sparrow.

He was half standing before he knew what he was doing. Eve bit his shoulder at the same time Brach yanked him violently back. The rustling of the bush's leaves seemed loud after so much silence, but Prince Nevan's party was already moving eastward. Nobody noticed except the Morvish witch, who shook her head.

It wasn't time for their spirit's plan to unfold. Moving too early could have dire consequences; she knew it as well as he did. Afterall, as Prince Nevan's horse began to move, she didn't fight the tug at her throat. She went willingly. Her smile was knowing, her wink flaring the color of the fate line between them. Given time, that line would thicken until it was ripe, and when it did, Kailevi would come back for her.

Prince Nevan would feel the wrath of a Thorne.

CHAPTER FOUR

THE SENTIENT FOREST

THERE WAS SOMETHING FOREBODING ABOUT THE SKY-SCRAPING tower nestled between mountains. It was one of two, Brach explained, standing on either side of a gorge so wide and deep it made the Long Gorge look like a crack in the sidewalk.

They called it the Womb.

Kailevi was noticing a trend—the Heart Lake, the Northern and Southern Spine, and apparently somewhere in the southeast there was also a Soul Lake. The mountain clan treated the land as if it were truly the Mother's body, respecting and cherishing it with prayer regularly. Some outright cried when they passed an unnatural clearing where humans had logged the land, pressing hands against the bleeding stumps to encourage fresh growth. It truly was incredible to witness fresh sprouts pushing up between their fingers, and Brach explained again how the fae would eventually come to heal it properly. Truly, the witches in this part of Nir were some of the most devout he'd ever met.

In comparison, the towers by the Womb were offensive. A necessary eyesore. Suspended between them hung a bridge that, if traveling by foot, was one of the only ways to cross from east to west. Not with wagons, though. There had to be a million stairs on either side, which made the crossing borderline inaccessible. Brach spoke of a ground-level option via a pass through the Southern Spine on the other side of Anfar, but the terrain was severe, the weather brutal. Only during the peak of summer could it be navigated, meaning that petitioning the Sparrow Coven for permission to use the towers was far safer.

For someone who had never left the confines of his home city, it was a lot to take in.

Once they'd passed the western tower, the forest began to change. Vertlyn's bright, open dryness was left behind as trees thickened, the ground no longer sharp with thistle, but lush and soft. Cursing Brach hadn't made walking without his boots easier, but it did prod the scout to take pity on him, fashioning makeshift shoes out of bandages and strips of leather.

There was so much green. It wasn't yet the beautiful rolling hills and misting waterfalls he'd dreamed of, but the change was promising. It was also sobering. For all the forest seemed to come to life, it was also darker, the height of the trees and their thick canopy limiting sunlight's reach. The hair on his arms stood up, a shiver running down his spine. They were getting close to Anfar, but it didn't feel any safer than Vertlyn had been.

Eve squirmed. Kailevi took her off his shoulders to carry in the crook of his arm instead, but it didn't ease her restlessness. Barking sharply, much to the annoyance of the mountain clan, she writhed until Kailevi had no choice but to drop her.

"Eve," he snapped.

His familiar had sprinted half a dozen feet back the way they'd come, every hair on her body fluffed out, teeth bared, her growl muffled by the fernery.

"Eve?" Kailevi knew how Eve behaved when danger lurked—

protective and aggressive, the way small dogs with big egos could be. This was not that. Hunkering low to the ground, she quivered with primal fear. "Eve, come here."

"It's Anfar's wards," Brach explained, stalking onwards, leaving Kailevi behind. "The territory is off-limits to fae and beasts, sans the dryads, of course. Did I not mention that?"

"No, you didn't," Kailevi muttered, closing his eyes.

Every time he checked the silver fate line winding around his finger, it was brighter. He was *so close* to where he needed to be. But he couldn't leave Eve behind. Couldn't stop here, either. Couldn't go back. The urgent tugging on his soul was violent enough to feel like panic.

Crouching in the soft grass, he ran his fingers through Eve's sandy fur.

"Give me a minute to figure this out."

Eve's growls quieted to a whimper; Kailevi wasn't going to abandon her.

The request had been in part for Brach as well, but the scout was already gone. The Northern Mountain Clan didn't wait. Frowning, Kailevi watched the last wagons disappear into the darkening forest.

He'd grown used to the quiet over the last week or so, but being alone in it was considerably less comfortable. The low hum of insects and distant songs of birds were the only signs that Kailevi and Eve weren't the last living things in the world.

If he'd been overwhelmed by the vastness of Nir before, he was outright panicking at the idea of being alone in it. Night would fall in the next hour, and he did not want to encounter anything on this side of Anfar's wards without the protection of the clan.

"Any ideas?" he asked Eve, who rested her chin on his boot and whined again, flicking her tail, sending sand *everywhere*.

Scowling, he brushed it into the grass. "Stop that. You're leaving a trail."

As if he'd offered her a pot of honey, she perked up and flicked her tail again, spinning in circles until there was a huge pile of it.

"Eve!" he hissed, desperately trying to disperse the mess.

The sand sprite nipped his hand repeatedly until he stopped. Sucking on the wound, he glared furiously. Eve didn't care, continuing her dance until she had a good pile. Slowly, deliberately, making sure she had his attention, Eve pawed at the ground three times, leaving three lines. His familiar grinned and cocked her head, as if any of that was supposed to mean something.

"Three?" Kailevi frowned.

Yipping, Eve pranced for a minute before tapping one line insistently.

"One of three?"

Again, she yipped excitedly.

Okay. He could figure this out. He knew that three and seven were special numbers often used in Morvish magic, hence why there were twenty-one seats on the council despite only twenty being filled, why there were seven academies in every city, their learning broken into three stages. It was why covens were only made in threes.

Covens.

He was one of three.

Kailevi closed his eyes, swallowing against the lump growing in his throat.

Way-finding might have lead him here, but it wasn't going help him get Eve through barring wards. He wasn't limited to way-finding, though. Coventry had strengthened the very little skill he'd had in dream-weaving, thanks to his bond with

Moyra. It had strengthened his abysmal skill in spell-cleaving, too.

His heart ached. Counting slowly, he measured his breaths.

Olyvia had died getting him into southern Nir. A part of the hurt was knowing that she hadn't needed to. Saving herself would have ruined him and Moyra, but if Olyvia had chosen to suck their entire pool of power into her body, she may have survived the unraveling of her soul. She hadn't, though. She had ripped open the wards and let the spell rip her apart, too. She'd left the pool for him and Moyra, and in that way, she was still with them. Olyvia had gotten him past Nir's wards, and she was going to get him through Anfar's too.

"Come on," Kailevi said, standing.

Trusting him, Eve let him tuck her into the crook of his arm again, suffering through her fear as Kailevi approached the invisible line between Vertlyn and Anfar. When she couldn't bear it anymore, biting him viciously in her carnal need to stop, Kailevi dropped his pack and put his familiar down. She curled up tight, tucking her nose beneath her tail, shivering against the power of the wards.

Pulling the box from his pack, he took out a point of clear quartz and a chunk of raw citrine.

"Eve," he called gently, offering her the golden ore. "Take this."

Peeking out from behind her tail, she whimpered, shuddering as she crept close enough to take the gemstone in her mouth. His familiar was in pain. Determination formed a ball of energy at his solar plexus.

"I won't be able to do this for long, so when I tell you to go, you go, okay?"

Sitting straight, legs crossed, he took the quartz and held it against the energy coiling in his stomach. Spell-cleaving was not a magic that came naturally to him, but he knew how to do it. Could probably break a hole in the wards long enough to let Eve slip through. It wouldn't break entirely, but the fact that he could do it at all was a miracle he attributed to his sisters.

Anchoring himself, embracing the disembodiment that came with opening up to Morvia, he let her realms untangle his mind from his body, his soul floating in the space between. He felt for the wards, sensing the magic like a wall of outward aggression. Whoever had made this had been violent and angry, but not stupidly so. They knew exactly what they were doing, and they did it with unabashed certainty.

"Spirit of stars, master of the moon, keeper of order—give me strength." Lifting his face, Kailevi kept his voice low lest anything nearby decide his vulnerability was a good opportunity for a snack. "I claim what is mine and refuse what is not; remove this barrier and let your will unfold."

He repeated it three times, lifted the quartz over his head, a spear to the sky. Energy rippled through his body, and he drew in as much of the pool as he dared, keeping his intentions clear in the front of his mind.

A sob cracked his chest open as he whipped his body forward, arms and crystal slicing through the air. His knuckles took the brunt of the impact as he hit the ground and felt the magic shooting forward, cutting through the wards like a blade.

"Eve, go!"

The moment he let go of the crystal, the little hole he'd made would close up, but every second he held onto it was drawing on the pool. Moyra would feel it, and he could imagine her terror.

Eve barked and Kailevi dropped the crystal, panting as the vibrations in his soul slowed, body tingling with pins and needles. Wiping the sweat from his face, he looked to where Eve stood to attention a dozen feet deeper in the forest. His smile was shaky as he sipped from his depleting store of ginseng tea. It wasn't enough to shake the exhaustion from his bones, but he climbed to his feet regardless and stumbled into Anfar.

~

Carrying the pervasive scent of moss and leaf rot, the air grew heavier the deeper they roamed. The sounds of fauna were absorbed by the oppressive atmosphere; even Eve was silent as they made their way around trees wider than their academy dorm room. The leafy canopy was so high overhead that Kailevi had to strain his neck to see the tightly interlocked branches blocking out the sky. Ferns dripped with moisture and large boulders blanketed in lichen and fungi crowded the forest floor, making every step treacherous. Yet, the darker it grew, the more there was to see.

Kailevi caught himself holding his breath as barked faces peered from within the trees—dryads silently watching the intruders. Some of the mushrooms growing from fallen trunks had a faint luminescence to them, as did the moss underfoot, leaving a trail of glowing footsteps in their wake.

"We're certainly not in Ahrenhale anymore, are we?" he muttered.

Shivering, Eve's ears flattened.

Hours had passed and night had fallen since they'd crossed into Anfar but they had not yet found the Northern Mountain Clan. Eve had taken them in circles trying to follow their scent and when Kailevi tried to use the fate lines as a guide, his head began pounding, his magic too hazy to grab hold of. Opening the wards for his familiar had taken more out of him than he'd thought.

There may not be many fae within the wards, no beasts, yet

it didn't feel any safer than the Heart Lake had been. *Something* lived in this forest. He'd narrowly avoided stepping in animal droppings too large to belong to anything as benevolent as deer or foxes.

Not even the stars provided security, the canopy was too tightly knit to see them. Fate lines ran strong through the trees but stretched untold distances, confirming that he was, for all intents and purposes, alone. Moyra's presence in his soul wasn't much of a balm. In fact, he could feel her pulling small amounts of magic from the pool—a distraction he didn't need.

Maybe it was time to find somewhere to wait out the night. He was hungry, Eve was hungry, and his feet were killing him. Also, leaving an obvious trail in the glowing moss for predators to follow was a bad idea. No doubt the mountain clan had made camp for the night too, so it wasn't as if he could fall farther behind.

Looking around at the wide trunks, the fallen logs as tall as he was, the boulders and rocks scattered around, so out of place that the only explanation he could think of was that stone giants must have cried them out during a world-crossing, he didn't see an obvious place to rest. The only time he'd ever camped in the wilderness was with the Northern Mountain Clan, and he'd had Brach to pitch their tent for him.

In the end, it didn't matter. The gentle suckling of Moyra's pull on the pool intensified, suddenly and violently, into a vacuum that sent Kailevi to his knees. Fingers digging into his stomach, grabbing hold as if he could pull Moyra through, shield her against whatever was happening, he gasped painfully for breath. Somehow, this was worse than when Olyvia had drawn on their coventry at the mountains. Moyra wasn't pulling to amplify her own power—she was hunting for one of theirs.

This far from Ahrenhale, there was nothing he could do to

help. Regret was gold and rose-quartz pink, and Kailevi didn't need blue pears to know what it tasted like.

When the vacuum on his soul didn't settle after a few minutes, he succumbed to the fact that this mossy spot on the forest floor was where he was going to stay.

Carefully, Eve curled up against his chest, staring, unblinking, eyes aglow with magic. Kailevi knew this trick; his familiar was not just a cuddly companion, after all. Thanking her, silently promising to find her some honey as soon as could, Kailevi let his familiar hypnotize him, soothing away a little of the pain and panic rife in his belly.

It was hours before he woke up.

He could only tell by the stiffness in his neck and might not have at all—the slow siphoning of energy in his gut told him Moyra was balancing precariously on the line of taking what magic she needed without draining him dry—but Eve had released him, growling with a malice Kailevi had never heard from her before.

They weren't alone.

Slowly, Kailevi sat up. The witches watching him were not from the Northern Mountain Clan.

It was difficult to see them in the dark, the soft blue luminescence from the moss and mushrooms casting deep shadows across their faces. What he could see, though, was filthy rags and matted hair, their skin darkened with soil. Their mouths were stained with something dark, too—with their mouths closed, the shadows made it look like a gaping hole in their face, but one of them was grinning, teeth glinting. Nothing about them was reminiscent of the soft, spinning girl of his dreams, so he doubted this was the Anfar Forest Clan he was meant to be finding. No, there was a distinct wildness to their appearance, a feral gleam in their eyes. Distantly, the four of them reminded Kailevi of the untrained witches lined up outside his parents' apothecary, but a glance at their auras warned him otherwise.

He swallowed the nervous lump in his throat and raised his hands. "I mean no harm."

Tilting their head, the closest one muttered something in a language full of long vowels and longer hisses. It was vaguely like how the Northern Mountain Clan spoke, but not quite. Terranian, but a different dialect, perhaps.

"Nirnish?" he asked.

Silently, in unison, the four witches drew stone knives from within their rags. The nearest one licked the blade, then pointed it at him.

"No harm," he tried again, fingers spread wide, pleading. "I have . . ." What did he have? What could he offer them?

Their auras flared and the witches began to fan out, circling, the nearest crouching low, ready to lunge, and Kailevi knew the answer was *nothing*.

He didn't know how to fight. The scuffles he'd gotten into at the academy had not prepared him for this. Scrambling to his feet, he grabbed for the nearest fist-sized rock; there was only time to do so because Eve's threatening growls morphed into a violent frenzy as she pounced for the nearest witch, whipping her tail, sending a spray of sand into their face.

The warmth of a body nearby was his only warning. Raising his arm, pain flared from his wrist to elbow as stone broke skin. Throwing the entire weight of his body, he shoved the witch back, turning to swing his rock at another creeping up behind him. Someone was screeching. Eve's rage was muffled by the mouthful of flesh she was tearing off a witch's hand and Kailevi's head swam with fear as they flung their arm, battering his familiar against a tree.

Heat burned his side a second before he registered the pain, and then he was on the ground. The witch on top of him ripped the blade from his gut, pinning his arms with her knees, the weight of her crushing his chest. Bucking in a mad attempt to throw her off, panic swelling as the bloodied knife tip rested against his throat, he screamed his familiar's true name. There wasn't anything the sand sprite could do, but feeling the fire in their bond was a comfort he needed as the final seconds of his life dawned closer.

Eve yipped, and Kailevi turned to look, forgetting for a moment the drag of the blade against his skin. The witch he thought might be their leader had his familiar by the throat, squeezing tight and grinning as Eve squirmed.

"Let her go," Kailevi begged. "Kill me if you have to, but let her go."

Curious, the witch tilted her head at him.

A hissed conversation began, Kailevi's captor tightening her grip on the knife at his throat. It took every scrap of his self-control for Kailevi to hold still, to prove his surrender, still quietly begging for his familiar's life. Eve's hind legs were losing the strength to kick and scratch, the witch's arm in bloodied ribbons. The shade of dripping wounds matched the dark shadows around her mouth and Kailevi lost control of his bladder as it occurred to him why these witches were so unnecessarily violent.

"Please," he asked again.

The conversation ended. Trembling, Kailevi lay perfectly still as the witches converged around him. Eve's feet were twitching, her eyes closed; if she was going to live, they had to let her go *now*.

"Please."

Crouching low, the witch holding Eve considered him. Lifted

the sprite between them.

"Please."

Eve's soft tail brushed against Kailevi's sweat-slicked skin as the witch brought the sprite to his face, pressing their noses together in a mockery of a kiss. Another plead sat on the tip of his tongue, frozen, heavy and burning as the crack of Eve's neck replaced the sound of his heartbeat.

The witch released her clenched fist.

Eve's body disintegrated in a cascade of sand.

It was in his nose. On his lips.

Kailevi thought he knew the pain of a broken bond. The body-shredding agony of it had almost knocked him out cold when Olyvia passed.

This was different.

His soul, his magic, was bound to his sister's, but his *everything* had belonged to Eve. It was a drop of blood given freely in exchange for a faerie's unbreakable promise—a cosmic claiming witnessed by the stars. She was *his* and he was *hers*, and now she was nothing but sand.

Kailevi was crumbling. There was no breath in his lungs, but he did not want for it. His heart was still beating, but he could not feel it. Only hear it, *crack, crack, crack*ing. The little life left in his body released in a single sob as he closed his eyes and waited for it to be over.

The suffocating forest swallowed the sound of his grief. It couldn't, however, smother the fern-shaking interruption of a furious growl.

Kailevi had watched Eve die with his own eyes, and yet, hope bloomed in his chest. The knife at his throat lifted and Kailevi followed the stares of the wild witches, frozen with terror.

Not Eve. Of course it wasn't Eve. If Kailevi had half a brain he would have known that his familiar could never have made a sound so deep.

The sound grew louder, awaking some primal need to *run*. A need amplified tenfold as a monster stalked out from behind a boulder.

It was not fae—*couldn't* be, here in Anfar—but it was no animal either, despite its proportions: wolfish, except too large, too muscular, like a bear. It wasn't entirely mammalian though. Scaled like a lizard, neck frill flared and undulating, thick black claws turned the earth with every threatening step forward. Fangs bared, its shiny black eyes were wholly focused on the witches.

The one who'd killed Eve spoke, and maybe Kailevi was starting to unravel, starting to lose his mind, because he could have sworn she was speaking to the wolf. Could have sworn the beast's next violent growl was a reply.

Kailevi blinked, and the witches were gone.

He couldn't feel his body. Hadn't realized the weight pinning him down had lifted until the shadowed canopy high overhead came into focus. The dirt and moss surrounding him was undisturbed; aside from the blood pooling beside him, leaking from his arm and side, there was no sign the witches had ever been there.

The lizard-wolf stalked toward him.

"Mother have mercy," Kailevi prayed.

Rather than tearing flesh and agonized screams filling the silent forest, the sound of squelching forced Kailevi to sit up and pay attention.

He had absolutely lost his mind.

The lizard-wolf had turned into wet clay, its body shifting and reforming into something humanoid. When the clay hardened again, another witch stood over him, completely naked, retaining the beady black eyes of the beast.

Kailevi blinked, then blinked again. Were the mushrooms in this forest hallucinogenic? Was the moss? He hadn't eaten any, but perhaps the toxin was airborne.

The witch walked away. A shaky breath left his body.

Sitting up was a challenge, but he managed it, grimacing at the lancing hot pain in his side and arm. Both hands were stained with blood but, wiping his face, he didn't care. It was preferable to the sand stuck to his skin.

His chest hitched, but before the internal pain could overshadow the external, the witch returned. Kailevi flinched back against a fallen log, fingers searching blindly for another rock. When had he dropped the first one?

Slowly, the witch raised her hands to show him the strips of moss she'd collected. She hissed words at him, but when he stared blankly at her, she tried a different language. When he still didn't understand, she tried Nirnish.

"What about now? Do you understand me now?"

Kailevi nodded.

"Good. This is for your wounds. Bleeding will attract predators."

"What are you?" he asked.

"Witch. What are you?"

"I've never seen a witch turn into a . . . a . . ."

"Lupanis," she said. "A beast native to the northwest. And no, you wouldn't have seen that spell before unless you know any other Mother-blessed witches. Which you don't, because there aren't any."

She was talking, but Kailevi could barely hear her. Flies were buzzing in his ears, ants crawling on his lips. He didn't have the strength to do anything, staring stupidly as the witch approached, wrapping a strip of moss around his arm and padding his side with another.

"Were you traveling with the Northern Mountain Clan?" she asked, audible now that she was right by his face.

Kailevi nodded.

"Not one of them, though. Can't be Terranian if you managed to get lost, and any Igni-blessed would have set the forest on fire before letting those cannibal rogues get so close." She took his hands, flipping them over to inspect his palms. "Not unbound." Moving his head to inspect the back of his neck, she hummed. "Not demi-kin." Black eyes appraising, she sniffed the air around him. "Not human, either. Born wild?"

Somewhere deep in the back of his mind, he recalled the high priest's advice. He didn't know what being born wild meant, but he couldn't admit to being Morvish. This witch, with her dirty reddish-brown curls and dangerous aura, wasn't exactly what Kailevi imagined a Sparrow witch to look like, but he couldn't be sure.

So he nodded, bracing himself.

The witch hummed again, scanning the forest. "Very generous of them to let you tag along. What did you offer them?"

"Nothing," he managed as sensation returned to his face. He'd stopped losing blood.

She didn't believe him. Eyes narrowing, she looked to the pack abandoned in the moss where, less than twenty minutes ago, he'd been deep in a sleeplike trance. Remembering why, Kailevi sucked in a breath and searched for his bond with Moyra. It was there, intact. The vacuum on his soul was still there but it was gentle again. He could manage it.

Misunderstanding his gasp, the witch moved to put herself

between the pack and him. "What can you offer *me* for guiding you back to the clan's camp?"

"Anything," he said, too quickly. This witch wasn't fae, but it was still foolish.

What other options did he have, though? He was lost, and Eve was . . . Eve was gone.

Before he could finish forming the thought—*coming here was a mistake*—the fate lines flared so brightly Kailevi was temporarily blinded. The golden thread around his finger tugged ferociously, and, strangely, so did the one between him and the shape-shifting witch. It was a different, though—purple instead of gold, and thin, like the one connecting him to the Morvish witch in Vertlyn. The pull was more a promise than a demand, enticing him to follow it to a future more pleasant than the one in store if he refused her aid.

Leaving him, the witch went to his pack and rifled through it, tossing aside clothes and books in favor of rifling through his box of crystals. While she looked, he grabbed one of his spare shirts, using his foot to hold it down so he could rip off the sleeve. The moss was cooling the wound, but hot blood still oozed through, so he wrapped the sleeve around his arm and bound it tight. Getting the rest of his shirt tied around his waist wasn't easier.

The shapeshifter pulled the citrine from his box, inspecting it closely. "This is good quality."

It better be, given what he paid for it. "Take it."

Nodding, the witch tied a curl around the raw crystal, creating a little hammock for it.

Focusing on the sting of his wounds, he refused to think about the way Eve had held that crystal in her mouth earlier that day. Refused to think about how, if he wasn't such a coward, if he'd just left her behind or sent her back to Qiri, she'd be alive right now.

Grinning, the witch replaced his belongings, threw his pack at him, and helped him to his feet. They took a single step before she stopped.

"Definitely not Terranian," she grumbled. "You cannot walk that loudly if you want to live."

"I . . . I can't walk any quieter."

For a moment, the witch was so still and so silent as she glared into the surrounding shrubbery that Kailevi began sweating again, waiting for the next murderous thing to come barrelling their way.

"You can. I will teach you," she finally said, slow and hesitant, "and in exchange, when we reach the trading festival, you will sneak me in."

"Sneak?" Kailevi asked. "You can't just . . . go?"

"No," she barked, and Kailevi thought he could see the deadly lupanis crawling beneath her skin as she turned her glare on him. "And no more questions. You either do it, or I leave you here to die."

He did not argue that, if she abandoned him, then she had technically stolen the citrine from him. He just agreed.

"I don't know how to sneak you in," he warned.

"Don't you worry about that," she said, violence melting into a smirk. "Now, pay attention. Terra's blessing may make walking without impact instinctive, but this is, first and foremost, Mother's land, and we are Mother's creatures. Your flesh and bones are made of the same cosmic dust as soil and stones. Feel it, and become part of it. Walk, knowing that you belong here."

He didn't, though. He didn't belong in this forest, with its silent, curious faces staring out at him. He didn't belong in this place where everything was trying to eat everything else. He didn't feel like Mother's creature at all—he was and always had belonged to Morvia.

To fail, though, was an insult to Olyvia. To lay down on the ground and let himself die was an insult to Eve. He couldn't allow himself to offend them any more than he'd allow a stranger, and so he closed his eyes and let go. He let go of the stars, of constellations, of threes and sevens.

He let go, and he walked.

CHAPTER FIVE

GREEN GIRL

THE WOUND IN HIS GUT THROBBED WITH EVERY STEP, BUT after weeks of travel, he'd grown accustomed to it. He was out of clean shirts to bandage himself with, though, and they hadn't been able to find fresh moss for a few days. Anxiety had been his constant companion as the hours, days, weeks passed by without any sign of the Northern Mountain Clan, but the witch named Kaelean promised they were going the right way. The possibility that she was leading him into a trap niggled in the back of his mind, but Kailevi had no choice but to follow her.

They stopped when they heard the voices.

Closing his eyes, Kailevi leaned against the nearest tree and breathed through the relief. By the time he'd composed himself, the witch was gone and there was a field mouse sitting on his foot, staring up at him.

"Okay, then. Thanks, I guess."

The mouse bit him. Hissing at the critter and at the ache in his side as he reached down, he scooped up it up and put it in his pocket.

"Do not bite me again," he whispered.

Sun filtered through the canopy high above but even so, the forest was more gray than green. The trees were larger, roots thicker as they twisted through the earth, and there was a chill to the air that did nothing to dilute the scent of leaf rot and damp soil. He'd thought things would brighten the deeper they went, but they hadn't, and as he made his way through the thick fernery toward the excited chatter of the festival, he prayed to Morvia that he was where he needed to be.

The familiar brown of the Northern Mountain Clan's leathers were a sight for sore eyes. They were mingled among a large crowd of witches dressed in cottons of varying shades of cream, green and grays, perusing lanes of wooden stalls filled with a variety of wares. Fruits and vegetables in above-perfect condition, clay pottery more beautiful than anything made in Ahrenhale, flowers more vibrant and fragrant than should be possible—Kailevi glanced at all of it, then moved on, searching for a familiar face.

A rustle in his trousers gave him pause. The mouse in his pocket squirmed free, dropping to the flattened earth and scurrying under the nearest stall. Kailevi was glad to be free of her. He was less glad when, fifteen minutes later, he was still wandering the lanes and surrounded by strangers. Brach could be anywhere—not that Kailevi was desperate to find him after the mountain witch abandoned him at the Vertlyn border, but it would be nice to recognize even one of the thousands of witches gathered. As for the green girl he'd come all this way looking for . . . Almost everyone here was green.

Finding a quiet spot between two stalls, Kailevi removed himself from the crowd, taking a moment to catch his breath. Wandering the festival was as likely to lead him to the right place as his aimless tromp through the forest had been, and though he'd recovered his strength, the fate lines were hazy and twisted. There was some kind of interference, the flavor of Morvish magic tainting all the Terranian prickling his skin. He needed something to help focus through it—ironically, he needed a tattoo.

There was no point wishing for things he didn't have. So, he looked at what he did have, instead.

Ever since the attack in the forest, the thread binding him to Moyra had been quiet. Weeks had passed, yet she hadn't come to find him in the dreamscape, either to check on him or explain why she'd had to siphon so much of their magic. His dream-weaving was only slightly better than his spell-cleaving, meaning he wasn't confident in reaching out to her without getting lost, so he had no way to know if she was okay. But, as he closed his eyes and drew on her magic, he hoped that wherever she was, she felt him, and knew that he was thinking of her.

He remembered what green tasted like, remembered petrichor and waterfalls and sunflowers. The dreamscape warped to take him back to those visions, just for a moment, so he could remember how it had felt to first lay eyes on the green girl. There was a tug in his chest, and when he looked back at the crowd, the fate lines were clearer. Webbing through the crowd in a rainbow of colors, all with their own interpretations, he sorted through them until he found the lone silver thread.

Trying to walk without jostling anyone was a dizzying task with one eye in the dreamscape to keep the fate lines focused, but he managed to ease back into the stream of people without too much trouble. He followed the silver line around stall after stall, down into a lane that offered more bones than pottery, the smell of herbs thickening until his eyes watered.

Sunflowers. He stopped dead in his tracks as he spotted it, apologizing to the people who squawked behind him. Hands turning clammy, he weaved his way back out of the stream, eyes locked on the glimpses of yellow flashing between bodies. When he finally broke through, he was at a stall for herbs, tonics and salves. A small laugh bubbled and died in his throat—of course the green girl from his dreams ran an apothecary. Of course.

She was exactly how he'd envisioned. The sunflower dangled heavily from a piece of twine being used as a necklace, bright against the sun-kissed brown of her skin. Mousy curls were bundled into a ponytail that trailed halfway down her back, her gauzy white skirt fluttering in the breeze. Finishing her conversation with a patron, she turned to him and smiled, amber eyes shining.

She greeted him in Terranian. Kailevi swallowed a curse.

"Do you speak Nirnish?" he asked, praying silently.

"Oh. Only a little."

Thank the gods.

"Great." For a moment, he could do nothing but stand there and breathe. Stare. He'd made it. He was here, and now he had no idea what to say.

"Are you looking for something?" she asked, hand hovering over a basket of herbs. "These are all blessed, of course."

There was definitely a language barrier, because he had no idea what she meant by blessed. Herbs couldn't be blessed by the spirits; they were herbs.

"Um." His mouth was dryer than the desert, and he tried to take a calming breath. He *could not* screw this up.

He was saved from having to come up with something to say when the girl gasped, reaching across the stall to grab his wrist. "You're hurt."

"Ah. Yeah. Had an encounter with some . . . ." Wracking his brain for the terms the shapeshifting witch had used, he hoped he sounded natural calling the cannibals "rogues."

Frowning, the pretty witch guided him behind her stall and carefully peeled back the bandages, exposing the long cut. "Not infected," she noted. "When did this happen?"

"A couple of weeks."

Her frown deepened, carefully prodding at the pinked skin on either side of the open wound. "This should be healed by now. What caused it?"

"A stone knife. I've been cleaning it, protecting it with moss I found in the forest, but it's not getting better."

"Probably a cursed blade," she muttered before dipping a finger into a nearby mortar filled with ground herbs moistened with blood. Using the mixture to draw a spellmark on her forehead, the witch closed her eyes and took Kailevi's arm in both hands. Quietly, lips barely moving, she muttered in Terranian until the air crackled with energy. Kailevi's stomach churned, nausea rising quickly, but he was able to push it down as he watched, wide-eyed, as the wound on his arm began to close.

"How . . ." he breathed, shaking his head as the cut closed completely, leaving only a pink line behind, and then, not even that.

The witch let out a slow breath, rolling her shoulders before inspecting her work. Catching Kailevi's stunned stare, she grinned.

"I take it you haven't seen the Sanni-blessed at work before?"

"Sanni-blessed . . ." He was not familiar with the smaller spirits. He was supposed to be, had studied them, but as soon as class was over the information flew out of his head. They weren't relevant to witches outside the wards, and at the time, the idea of crossing them had been inconceivable.

It was a blunder, though. The witch tilted her head, smile fading.

"You don't know Sanni?"

"I . . ." He'd been warned not to tell, but he also didn't want to lie to her. "I do. That's the healing one." Obviously. "I just never paid attention in school. I . . . don't have that kind of magic."

"Ah." She smirked, disposing of the bloody rag he no longer needed to bandage his arm. "Which spirit did bless you, then?"

Again, he didn't want to lie, but he still had no idea what to say to her.

"That's complicated," he decided. "But thank you."

"Ellissa." She took his hand in both of hers and nodded.

"Kailevi," he returned. "Nice to meet you. But, if it's not too much to ask . . ."

He lifted the edge of his shirt to expose the second wound, which was healing much worse than the first. The blade had been much deeper in his gut.

Ellissa's eyebrows shot up. "I'm shocked you even made it here."

She had no idea.

"Me too." Kailevi grimaced as she removed the wad of cloth he'd tied around his waist. "I had some help."

"And where is that help now?" she asked, distracted as she poked his tender skin.

Gods, her hands were warm.

Closing his eyes, forcing himself to stop thinking about her hands, he considered what to tell her. The wild witch who'd saved him clearly didn't want anyone to know she was here and Kailevi had a strong feeling that betraying her would not end well for him.

It wasn't a lie, though, when he decided to leave her out of it and said instead, "They died."

One day, he was going to have to sit down and face the pain

constricting his lungs. Refusing to blink, refusing to let the burning in his eyes overwhelm him, he watched Ellissa work her magic once again. The voice in his head that told him coming south had been a mistake, that he had destroyed his coven, his family, his familiar, out of selfishness and naivety, was quieter as long as he was looking at her.

Ellissa's touch was as gentle as her voice as she said, "May they rest well."

The platitude slowed the darkening of his thought. It was a surprisingly kind thing to say; nicer, in that it took the focus away from his loss and placed it on Olyvia and Eve's new home with the Lover.

Admiring her handiwork, Ellissa continued, "I understand. Many of my family have been embraced, reaching perfection more regularly than most. Here, we celebrate their passing—it is an honor to be chosen. As a gift from the Mother to her Lover, your friends have fulfilled their highest purpose. Be proud."

Something about that disturbed him, but he didn't argue. Not now. Besides, in a convoluted way he could understand how viewing death so optimistically could be easier than bearing it. So he repeated her words in his mind, over and over, trying to be glad for Eve and Olyvia rather than miserable for himself.

"Thank you, Ellissa."

"You're welcome. "

"Here," he said, lowering his pack and rifling through it until he found his box of crystals. "Can I give you one of these as payment for your services?"

"No, no, it's . . . What is that?" Her nose wrinkled as she picked out the jar of pickled pear.

Kailevi smiled. "Blue pear."

"*Blue* pear?" Curious, she unscrewed the cap and took a sniff.

"I have never seen these before. Do they grow in the Northern Mountains?"

He really ought to have given a single thought to what he was going to say when he arrived. Running a hand through his hair, he desperately tried to figure out how to explain.

"Um, not exactly."

The vague answer spiked suspicion; Ellissa straightened, furrowing her brow as she gave him a slow appraisal. It was the first time she'd looked at him, not as a potential customer or as the host of injuries, but as a person, and judging by the twist of her mouth, something about him was striking as off. His clothes were not of the mountain clan, and he was the only one in the whole forest wearing wraps on their feet. He did not blend in. It had not occurred to him to try and do so.

For a moment they simply stared at each other, unspoken words twisting the tension until Kailevi felt ready to snap. Lifting her chin, Ellissa scanned the nearby crowd, waiting for a couple of witches to move on from her stall before saying, "Night is not far. I have to go inside soon but, tomorrow, there will be music and dancing. Perhaps we could take a walk? You could show me the moss you used."

His relief was more nauseating than the magic she'd used on him. Could she sense it—the connection between them? Given the sorts of things he'd seen in the few weeks he'd been in southern Nir, his blundering should have alarmed her, yet Ellissa seemed carefully curious, unafraid of a secretive stranger.

If he didn't know better, he would swear Morvia was watching over him.

Kailevi smiled. "I would like that."

Night in the Anfar forest was chilly, even in summer, and the early morning light brought little relief. Kailevi had grown used to sleeping on the naked forest floor while traipsing through Anfar, but it had been pleasant to do so by the Northern Mountain Clan's campfires for a change. A few witches had given him funny looks as he'd settled by them, but he was too annoyed with Brach to ask around for him.

The downside of sleeping by campfire, though, was that he woke sooty and sweaty. A nearby pond was being used by the clan to freshen up, so he'd done his best to wash away the body odor and the worst of the dirt from his clothes, marveling at the flawless skin of his abdomen. It was as if he'd never been injured. Magic like that in Ahrenhale would earn a fortune, but Ellissa had just given it to him for free.

Relatively clean, he stood to the side as Ignatius-blessed witches prepared a bonfire for the day's celebrations. Flutists, fiddlers and drummers warmed their hands before testing their instruments, vendors setting up nearby with fresh produce.

"So."

The sudden sound made him flinch back, turning to find Ellissa standing behind him with an amused smirk on her face. Daisies were tucked into her braid.

"You know, I didn't survive a pack of rogues just to come here and have a heart attack," Kailevi grumbled, but he couldn't keep the smile off his face as he did.

"It wouldn't be fatal. I'm standing right here." Humor lit her eyes to a golden honey. Taking his hand, she nodded her chin away from the bonfire and led him deeper into the forest.

"Is it safe for us to move away from the festival?" Kailevi asked, trying to pay attention to the surrounding shrubbery despite the warmth of her hand.

"Anything with a brain won't be seen within a mile of a gathering this size," she assured him.

Still, they didn't go far. The music could still be heard when they stopped by a large, twisting root. Ellissa leaped with ethereal grace onto the lichen-crusted log, pacing along it slowly as she formulated her questions.

"You're not from the Northern Mountain Clan," she reiterated from their conversation yesterday. "And you don't seem to have brought anything to trade, so you're not a vendor, either."

"No. I was looking for someone and the clan let me follow them down."

"Who are you looking for?" she asked, watching him as he paced alongside the log with her.

Kailevi couldn't help it. His smile widened. "I wasn't sure."

Understandably, that confused her. They stopped their pacing as Ellissa sat down, spreading the length of her skirt around her, picking at loose cotton. Kailevi watched her think, losing the smile when all signs of humor left her face.

"Are you a Sparrow?"

"Gods, no."

He could not have answered quicker. Her relief was short lived.

"So, where are you from, then? You said it's complicated, but I can't think of anywhere that wouldn't teach you about the spirits."

Kailevi sighed. It was a risk to tell her the truth, but it was a risk he would take. Her obvious relief at him not being part of the Sparrow Coven was comforting. "I learned more about the major spirits. The minor ones don't have much impact on my people. I—"

"That doesn't make sense," she interrupted, shaking her

head. "You're definitely a witch, or else the mountain clan wouldn't have let you tag along. You *have* to be blessed, and it *must* be by one of the seven; Mother may bless us with children, but she doesn't give away her magic. The Lover is more generous, but you already said you weren't Sparrow. You can't be Morvish—they never leave their little bubble up north—"

He winced.

Ellissa noticed.

"Oh gods, you are, aren't you."

Bracing himself, Kailevi waited. He was either about to be in a world of shit, or about to have a very long conversation. But the silence lingered. Tension brought his shoulders up to his ears as he tried to convince himself to meet Ellissa's gaze. He felt it, hot on his skin.

"I won't tell anyone," she finally said, quiet. Then, a little more poignantly, she barked, "And the dryads are going to keep this to themselves, aren't they?"

Kailevi flushed. He hadn't thought of that.

"Shit."

"It's alright."

The comfort didn't mean much. He knew damn well that Morvish emissaries were going missing in Dusarn and now the gossipiest fae in the world knew about him.

"Being Morvish is not a very safe thing to be around here," he explained.

Ellissa already knew, her face apologetic and somber. "No, no it's not."

"Is Wyldeden close with the Sparrow Coven?"

"Furthest thing from it." That was a little more reassuring, until she continued. "But there are some elders who would jump at the chance to have a Morvish witch under their thumb. I'm sorry. I honestly didn't think you were, or I wouldn't have said anything. Aren't Morvish witches meant to have a tattoo on their foreheads?"

Kailevi sighed.

"Sorry. I'll stop asking questions. If it helps, you can ask me something super intrusive too."

He wanted to hear her questions—he wanted to tell her *everything*—but not here. It wasn't safe. More than that, though, he wanted to wipe the guilt off Ellissa's face.

"Alright," he agreed, trying and failing to suppress a smile. Stepping closer, he leaned against the log and rested his chin on folded arms. "Do you have a boyfriend?"

Ellissa scoffed, swinging her feet. "Seriously?"

"What? Too embarrassing?"

"Try cliché. And childish."

The first was the point, but the second stung a little. He wondered how old Ellissa was. Wondered if he ought to mention that he was still seven years from his quarter-century and full maturity.

"But," she continued with an exasperated sigh, "if you must know, I do not."

"Girlfriend?"

"No."

"Fun-buddy?"

Scandalized, Ellissa screeched, "*Fun-buddy?*"

Kailevi laughed, burying his face in his arms to smother the sound. By the time he composed himself, Ellissa was smiling again.

"A friend of mine coined the term back in Ahrenhale," he explained. "It was their preferred label."

Raising an eyebrow, she asked, "A *friend* friend?"

"Oh, is that the term used in Anfar? I must say, fun-buddy is much less confusing."

Ellissa spluttered for a while before throwing up her hands. "The point is, no, I don't have a . . . a . . . *fun-buddy*. I don't date."

Tilting his head, Kailevi could barely contain his relief. "No?"

"No. Most people are not very interesting."

She said it so dismissively that Kailevi couldn't help but fall into laughter again. His knees buckled under the weight of his chortling, only getting worse when Ellissa pinched him.

"Well, they're not!"

Righting himself, Kailevi wiped his face. "You and I know very different people."

"We do," she conceded. "Honestly, I just don't feel like wasting my time. When I date someone, I'm doing so with union in mind. If I'm going to spend the rest of my life with someone, I want them to at least not bore me straight into the Lover's embrace."

Kailevi laughed again, even as he felt his face heat. Union. He hadn't thought he was the type to marry young, but there he was, absolutely certain he was going to marry Ellissa one day.

At the end of every day, Ellissa asked if she could see him again in the morning, and every morning, they wandered the outskirts of the festival. She told him about Wyldeden, how it existed in a pocket carved out of Terra's realm. She told him about her family, her studies, her role in the clan. They talked about herbs and recipes for salves. Slowly, he started learning her language. When Ellissa mentioned her love for fruit, Kailevi took out the jar of pickled pears again. It took some encouragement but eventually she tried a bite, her eyes widening as the world came alive in a brand new way.

In return, he told her as much as he could, given the

likelihood of curious ears. He talked about the weeks traveling south, about his sisters, about Eve. He told her what it was like to see fate's web laid over the world, what it was like to manipulate dreams. He didn't say anything about the wards, not yet, but Ellissa knew when he was censoring himself and didn't push for details.

Time was a metronome that slowed for no one though, and soon, the week was over. The Northern Mountain Clan was packing up to begin the journey back to the Long Gorge and Kailevi was faced with the reality of being on his own again.

"You can't stay out here!" Ellissa screeched as he told her his plan.

"It'll be fine. I'll make a shelter, rig up some alarms."

"Absolutely not."

"Elly." He took her hands, warmed not only by them but by the protective heat blazing in her eyes. "I can't go back to the mountains. I can't walk away from you. We may barely know each other, but I want to change that."

His declaration did not scare her. "I want that too. But Kai, it isn't safe out here. I don't want to come out one day and find you gone."

"I promise to try very hard not to get killed by rogues," he said, but the joke fell flat.

"I . . ." Her voice, her hands, her breath—everything was trembling. Pulling her closer, he tucked her head against his shoulder. There, she steadied herself enough to speak. "I could petition to let you into Wyldeden."

That sounded ominous. "Is that . . . difficult?"

"The clan's been known to adopt wild witches every now and then. Not often, but it does happen. But, if the elders allow it, you'll have to live by our culture."

"I can do that."

Ellissa shook her head. "Without knowing where you come from, they will see you as low-blessed, and, if we decide on union, my family will not be welcoming to you."

"That's okay," he told her. "I can handle it."

Lifting her head, Ellissa searched his face. He didn't know what she was looking for, but if it was doubt, she wouldn't find it.

"Alright then." Her smile bloomed softly, and, overwhelmed with gratitude for Morvia's guidance, Kailevi pressed his lips against it.

MORNING

THE VERSION OF THE STORY KAILEVI TOLD HIS FAMILY WAS A
lot less bloody than it had been in reality. Everyone received a
happy ending. Eaon's wide-eyed curiosity had dampened some
time ago, his blinks turning long and slow, but he was still
fighting sleep with all the power in his tiny body. Pulling the
blanket up, Kailevi pressed a soft kiss to his son's forehead.

"That was quite a story," Ellissa whispered as the first rays of
dawn lightened the curtains.

"It was," Kailevi agreed.

"I liked how you turned me into a magical blue pear."

Grinning, he teased, "Those are real, you know."

"Oh, I know. Yet, they're not what you crossed the world to
find."

"No, they weren't." Leaning over carefully, aware of their
sleeping children between them, he pressed a kiss to her cheek.
"I was looking for you, my little peach."

Ellissa rolled eyes at him. An encouragement if he'd ever
seen one.

Kissing her again, he chuckled. "My sugar plum."

"Your food obsession is not endearing."

"Pretty petal," he tried instead.

A small thrill heated his blood as his wife turned ever so slightly, looking him dead in the eye, voice flat as she said, "Cabbage head."

Kailevi barked a laugh as hard as he had when Eaon had first said it—the only insult his four-year old mind could conjure after Kailevi made him bathe.

At the disturbance, Eaon shifted under the sheets, burying his head under Kailevi's pillow. Eavha stirred with a little sigh, bringing the room to a hush. They waited in pleading silence as their children drifted back to sleep.

Once they were certain quiet conversation wouldn't wake them, Ellissa carefully sunk back into the mattress. "We could visit one day, if you like."

Kailevi brushed his fingers through Eaon's curls. He couldn't imagine what it would be like to go back to Ahrenhale now. What would Moyra, who, judging by the strong but silent thread tying them together, was still alive and hating him, say if he just showed up out of the blue? Gatty would kill him.

"I don't know, Elly."

Outside, the rooster crowed.

"Kai." The humor was gone, buried under concern. "What if they grow up and they're not like my family? What if their magic is more like yours?"

It was something he had been afraid of since the day Eaon was born. There were no Morvish academies in Wyldeden, or anywhere in Nir as far as he knew. He couldn't exactly ask; exposing his true affiliation hadn't become less dangerous. If the Sparrow Coven found out he was here, that he had children, they'd stop at nothing to get ahold of them.

Kailevi searched for the purple fate line he'd discovered in Vertlyn again. It had swelled the day Eaon was born, and again when Eavha had arrived. He'd spent nearly every night since then trying to find that Morvish witch in the dreamscape, hoping to beg her to keep his children out of whatever tangled web she was trapped in, but in the thirty years since that day, he hadn't been able to find her again. Not without walking into Pirevia, which he was not about to do. He couldn't afford to get caught. Couldn't risk the Sparrow Coven finding out about Eaon and Eavha. If Morvia was cruel enough to bless them . . .

"I'll figure something out."

Ellissa was not convinced, but she didn't push. Instead, her fingers threaded through his, squeezing tight. "Do you miss it? Your home? The rest of the world? Your adventures?"

For a moment, he could almost taste indigo again. He could feel sand in his boots and the baking sun as he crossed the desert. The tickle of heather against his nose. Tiny claws in his chest.

Kailevi smiled and brought Ellissa's knuckles to his lips.

"I like this one more."

ACKNOWLEDGMENTS

I don't usually write an acknowledgment for novellas, and this one will be short, but there are two people in particular who need to be thanked for the existence of this story.

First, Kat, who has been my editor for 3+ years now. You loved Kailevi before I even thought he had his own story to tell, and it is only because of your interest that I explored this era in the chronicles at all.

Secondly, Samantha. This is the official acknowledgment that I owe you my second-born child. Thank you for being my sounding board.

Until next time!

Alex.

ABOUT THE AUTHOR

 Alex Clifford has spent the past decade studying creative writing, interior design, sociology, psychology and secondary education, bringing it all together to do what they have always loved to do best— tell stories. As a neurodiverse, queer, widowed, single parent, Alex is excited to bring their perspective and experience to the fantasy genre for many years to come.

For more on Alex Clifford's upcoming work, visit: www.alexclifford.com.au

You can find them on social media at:
Facebook: facebook.com/AfsCliffordBooks
Twitter (X): @AfsClifford
Instagram: @almost_alex
TikTok: @alexcliffordwrites

www.ingramcontent.com/pod-product-compliance
Lightning Source LLC
Chambersburg PA
CBHW011917130726
47904CB00015B/2757